Love Unfailing

A Divine Love Series
Book 2

by Tara Taffera

Copyright © 2021 by Tara Taffera
Published by Forget Me Not Romances, an imprint of
Winged Publications

Editor: Cynthia Hickey
Book Design by Forget Me Not Romances

This book is a work of fiction. Names, characters, Places,
incidents, and dialogues are either products of the author's
imagination or used fictitiously. Any resemblance to actual
persons, living or dead, or events is coincidental. Scripture
quotations from The Authorized (King James) Version.

Fiction and Literature: Inspirational
Christian Romance

ISBN: 978-1-956654-01-1

Chapter 1

Anna looked at the friends and family gathered around her mother's patio, and joy consumed her. Why then was there a gaping hole in her heart? She gazed over at her brother Christian and his wife Gina, who also happened to be Anna's best friend in addition to her sister-in-law. Those two depicted the picture-perfect postcard of happiness. And she wasn't jealous. How could she be when she knew of the grief they both endured when her brother Alex died, Gina's first husband? The horrific car accident that claimed his life, and her niece Teresa, took years for them to heal from. But, in the end, it brought Gina and Christian together.

Alex Jr. (AJ, as they call called him now) interrupted Anna's thoughts when he sprinted toward her. "Aunt Anna, look what Nana Helena gave me."

"Are those bubbles? Oh, I love bubbles. Your Dad and I used to blow those together when we were little."

"Really?"

"Yup, and we would chase them all over the yard."

"Will you do that with me, Aunt Anna?"

"I promise, but a little later, okay?"

He flashed a Titanic-sized smile that always reminded her of Alex and took off to the man he called Dad, his Uncle Christian. His dad in every way that mattered. Gina and Christian planned to tell him when he was old enough that Alex died when AJ was already in her womb—though she didn't know it at the time.

"Dad, Aunt Anna said when you guys were little, you used to chase bubbles around."

Christian's eyes moved to Anna, and he winked, knowing that was his brother and sister's thing, though Christian joined in from time to time.

"We did, buddy."

"She said we would blow bubbles later and chase them. Do you want to play with us?"

"You bet."

The boy's attention turned quickly to his mom and new baby sister, Evangeline, Eva for short. AJ was three now, and the kid never stopped smiling, especially when he was around the baby. Anna observed the four of them all huddled together. Though no one else would likely notice, despite the smile on his face, Anna glimpsed the worry that resided there as Christian looked down at his wife and whispered in her ear. She would wager money that Christian just asked if she was okay. The slight nod of Gina's head gave it away. Today was Gina's first big family gathering since Eva was born. She battled post-partum depression with Eva and with her first-born Teresa, so Christian worried about her incessantly.

"Hey, Anna, you look lost in thought. Making sure your brother doesn't hover over his wife all day?"

"Someone has to make sure he won't mess this up," she joked to her friend Elizabeth.

"Seriously, though, do you think she's okay?"

"Yes, we simply have to make sure she is surrounded by the people she loves and help her out when she needs it. With Christian back to work, a new baby, and AJ running around, it's got to be stressful."

"Well, that's one of the reasons I came over here. I'm planning a girls' night at my house on Friday with the three of us. You in?"

"Of course! We need one so badly."

"I know, we haven't gathered since Eva was born. So, bring on the junk food and the gossip."

Anna felt better already.

~

"Girls, I missed this so much," said Anna, as she dug her hand into the bowl of salt and vinegar chips.

"You? I have been dreaming of this," said Gina. "Well, maybe not dreaming since I hardly sleep anymore, which makes that impossible."

Elizabeth and Anna studied her—their faces etched with worry lines, even though neither of them hit the dreaded 3-0 yet.

"Stop looking at me like that, you two. I'm fine. It was a joke."

"I know, Gina, we just worry about you," said Elizabeth.

"And I love you guys for it, but I'm okay. I don't get out much. Tell me what's going on with you two."

"Anna went on a date the other night," Elizabeth blurted out.

"What? Why am I just now hearing about this?"

"Because it wasn't a great date."

"I still want all the gory details," Gina demanded.

"There is nothing to divulge. It was boring, just like the date before that and the date before that."

Gina and Elizabeth exchanged glances.

"What?"

"Nothing," said Elizabeth.

Anna threw a pillow at her.

"Listen, you guys, it's no picnic out there."

"Gee, I wouldn't know anything about that?" said Elizabeth. "Oh wait, no great dates for me either. Join the club, sister."

Now it was Gina looking over with a knowing glance and the hint of a smile.

"What?" the other two said in unison.

"Nothing."

They raised their eyebrows at her.

"Fine. You know what I'm going to say."

"God has a plan," said Elizabeth.

"So, you keep telling us," said Anna. "I just wish he would fill me in on what it is."

"Come on. Grace and I keep telling you two the right man is out there waiting for you."

"Speaking of Grace, why couldn't she be here tonight?" asked Elizabeth.

"I was just going to ask you that," said Gina.

"She has a date."

"Good for her," said Anna, "I hope it's better than mine."

Grace was old enough to be their mother, but they all became close a few years ago when the two met in Gina's grief group after Alex and Teresa died. Grace's daughter perished in a brutal murder, and she and her husband divorced sometime later. While Grace went to the group to heal, her husband retreated into himself. The walls he erected were too strong for Grace to knock down. Devastation gripped her when he dropped the divorce papers on the table one day. That was a few years ago, and this was just one of a handful of times she went out with another man.

"She is coming over tomorrow to help out with the kids," said Gina. "I will uncover the full scoop."

"Great, while you are at it, get a date from her for another get-together next week," said Anna.

"Perfect," said Gina. "I'll be the old boring married woman who has you three to fill me in your exciting dating lives."

This time, Anna and Elizabeth launched a throw pillow in her direction, and they all doubled over in laughter.

Chapter 2

"You really think Gina is doing okay? You don't think I need to go over there?" Helena asked for what seemed like the hundredth time that day.

"I told you, Mom, you need to stop hovering. Gina is fine. Just because she suffered in the past, we can't assume she will fall apart. I know you are a huge help, but you have to resist the urge to hover every day."

"I guess you're right."

"I'm sorry, what was that?"

Her mother ignored the comment while she continued to stir her mint tea mindlessly.

"How was your date the other night?"

Ugh, maybe she should have kept the conversation focused on Gina.

"I told you, Mom, it was fine."

"I'm sorry, Anna. I only want you to find someone and be happy."

"I am happy."

"You know what I mean. You're such an amazing person. I want you to discover that all-consuming love."

Her mother was exasperating, but she wanted the best for Anna, and she loved her for it.

"So, what's wrong with these men you go out with?"

"Mom!"

"What? I simply want to know what you're looking for."

"That's the thing. I'm not sure, but it's not forced conversation with these guys who I have nothing in common with."

Her mother patted her hand. "It will happen, honey. You just have to be patient."

"Well, while I'm waiting, can you maybe not ask me every day if I met the right guy?"

"Hmph," was her only answer.

"Listen, about dinner tomorrow. I know everyone always comes at 4, but you know the door stays open for you anytime."

Sunday gatherings at her mom's house were a staple for as long as Anna remembered. She often dreamed of a time when she would take over the tradition and host it with her own family.

"Anna, are you even hearing anything I'm saying?"

"Sorry, Mom. I will probably be there at 4. I'm going to church in the morning, and sometimes a few of us go out for lunch after."

"Oh, has Gina started going back to church already?"

"No, it's still too hard with the baby, but Elizabeth and I go together. I feel like I belong there."

Her mother's eyes darted back and forth, and Anna knew that sentence was being dissected to death, but thankfully she moved on.

"That's great. Maybe you will meet a nice man."

"Goodbye, Mother, see you tomorrow."

She walked down the steps with a smile on her face, despite her mother's interrogation. She did have her eye on someone, but he hadn't noticed her yet. The thought that maybe he would soon caused her heart to skip a beat.

Anna sat at church scanning the room for Elizabeth when she snuck up behind her.

"Where did you come from? I was staring at the door the whole time."

"Apparently not. Maybe you couldn't keep your gaze off the hunky guy on stage."

Anna nudged her in the arm, and she could practically feel the blush creeping up her tanned cheeks. The band was already playing before the service started in a few minutes.

"I lived in Florida my whole life; you think I would get used to this heat already," Elizabeth was saying. "Look at me. I need another shower just from the walk in here."

"I know, thank goodness for sundresses, right?"

"Yes, I noticed you are wearing a new one today. Any reason, in particular?"

"Elizabeth, seriously, I said the guy was cute. You know if you keep this up, I won't tell you stuff anymore."

"I'm kidding. I promise to be on my best behavior when we all have lunch after the service."

"What?"

"Garett is joining our group today. Oh, did I not mention that yesterday?"

Anna opened her mouth to protest, but the service started, and upbeat music reverberated throughout the sanctuary. Now she was the one who needed another shower.

~

Anna and Elizabeth walked along the waterfront in Tarpon Springs, home to the famous Sponge Docks, on their way to the restaurant they chose for today's lunch spot. It was a favorite among the locals—Greek, of course. The town was built by Greek immigrants, and Anna never tired of coming to the downtown area. She was proud to share that culture and live in this city full of such rich history. And, of course, she loved all the Greek delicacies. Thankfully, her mother could make any of the dishes found here in her sleep.

"Come on, Anna, I can't stroll around anymore. It's so humid. I have to get back in the air conditioning."

"Agree!"

"Anna, wait up!"

They both turned to see their friend Tony walking toward them.

"Fine, but you better hurry. We are melting over here."

"Seriously, it's crazy hot today, isn't it? Good thing our church is casual, so I could wear shorts."

Anna looked at Tony in his slim-fit shirt that hugged his chest and noticed she and Elizabeth weren't the only ones glistening with perspiration. From his thick dark hair to the wet dots around his brow, the heat evidently affected everyone.

"Hey, Tony," Elizabeth greeted him.

"Let's head inside and get a table and wait for everyone else. I'm melting."

~

Tony took a few brisk steps to get ahead and hold the door open for the two women. Elizabeth entered first, and when Anna followed behind, he noticed how pretty she looked in her floral dress, which fit like it was made just for her. Tony glanced inside and was surprised to see that everyone was already there, and three seats remained open for them. But they weren't together. Tony took the lone chair between two of his buddies from the singles group while Anna and Elizabeth grabbed those on the other side of the table. Before Anna sat down, Garrett leaped up to pull the chair out for her, then repeated the gesture for Elizabeth. Was it Tony's imagination, or did he only touch the small of Anna's back when he pushed her chair into the table? Tony saw the smile play on Anna's plump lips and couldn't believe another girl was falling for Garrett's charms. Yeah, the guy was good-looking, but seriously, he must spend all day in the gym to get arms like that. They basically busted out of his sleeves. That, and the fact that he led the band in church, kept all the young women swooning. Tony wasn't buying it, though. He experienced a weird vibe around him, and he didn't want him anywhere near Anna.

The group headed out together, and Tony immediately strode over to get closer to Anna, but Garrett got there first. Tony backed away but was still in earshot.

"Anna, I really enjoyed getting to know you a little today. Can I get your number and give you a call sometime?"

Tony witnessed the blush inch up her cheeks. Despite her complexion, the pinkish hue was still evident. It contrasted with her dark brown eyes, and Tony had to tear his gaze from her. He could get lost in her delicate features.

"Sure," was all she said. Tony visibly cringed when Garrett eagerly entered her number into his iPhone 11. When he hugged her goodbye, Garett's arms lingered too long on Anna's slender frame.

Anna walked back over to Elizabeth and Tony, the smile taking over her round face.

"Well, someone enjoyed lunch," said Elizabeth. "I want to hear all the details. Come on, let's walk over to that little place for coffee—iced, of course."

"Sounds good. I have nothing else going on today until dinner at my mom's."

She turned toward Tony. "Are you coming with us?"

Even though the last thing he wanted to hear about was her crush on Garrett, he could never turn down spending time with Anna.

"Sure, lead the way."

~

Anna couldn't wait for 7:00. Gina, Elizabeth, and Grace were coming over, and she was excited to tell them all about her group lunch with Garrett last Sunday. Elizabeth already spilled some details, but still, it would be nice to sit around with her friends, eat and gab together. With Gina so busy with Eva, their get-togethers happened less frequently.

Anna heard a knock and hoped it was Gina. She really missed her friend and sister-in-law. Sure, they saw each other often, but it was either at Sunday dinner, or her brother was always hovering around. He was utterly in love with her, but sometimes she wanted her friend to herself. Maybe that's why she was unlucky in love? Gina and Alex, and then Gina and Christian, set an impossibly high bar to strive for.

"Hey, Gina," she said, immediately pulling her into a hug. "I was hoping it was you. I never get to chat with you, just the two of us. I miss you!"

"Hey, Anna," was all she said in return. Anna spotted the dark circles under her brown eyes, and her dark hair stuffed haphazardly on top of her head in a messy bun.

"So, how's Eva?"

"She's amazing as ever. I'm just so exhausted. I would give you 20 bucks if you let me go upstairs and sleep right now, then tell Christian we all enjoyed a great time gabbing together."

"Seriously?"

"I won't, but that's how exhausted I am."

"Sleep here then tonight. Let Christian get up with the baby, and you can be home before he leaves for work."

"That sounds like heaven, but no."

"Why not?"

"Because I'm a mom, Anna. Moms just don't leave their kids to hide somewhere else."

Whoa, tell me what you really think. Her sister-in-law must be bone-tired, as she never snaps at her friends.

"But, Gina, you need some rest. I know you like to be superwoman, but sometimes even she needs sleep. I'm texting Christian right now to ask him."

"Stop, please don't. I don't want him to get mad at me."

"Why would he get mad at you? He loves you, Gina. You need a break."

The doorbell interrupted them, and Anna was glad Elizabeth and Grace both arrived.

"Hey, girls, come on in."

"You better not have started any gossiping about hunky Garrett without us."

Anna laughed at Grace, took their coats, and got everyone settled on the couch with a feast of appetizers and drinks on the table in front of them.

"Not yet. I was trying to get Gina to stay to get an uninterrupted night of sleep, but she refuses to give in."

"Gina, stubborn?" asked Elizabeth sarcastically.

"Very funny," she shot back. "You guys just wait until you have kids and realize what a luxury sleep is."

"That's why you need to take me up on my offer," said Anna.

"We'll see," she said while grabbing a coke, some pita bread with tzatziki sauce, and tomato and feta salad.

"So, Garrett's hunky?" started Gina.

While Anna didn't want to be teased endlessly about her crush, she was thrilled to see the smirk on Gina's lips, a reminder of the sister-in-law she loved so much. Anna was thankful to know she was still in there.

"Well, since you asked. Seriously, you should see his biceps. And you know how I always said he looked like a body builder? Well, guess what, at lunch, he told me he is! He sometimes enters competitions on the weekends."

"What? We have got to meet this guy," said Grace.

"Oh, we are definitely not there yet."

"So, where exactly are you?" coaxed Elizabeth. "You looked deep in conversation during lunch."

"Yeah, it was nice getting to know him. We texted a lot this week, but he hasn't asked me out yet. He told me he would see me at church on Sunday."

"Elizabeth, was it me, or is Tony not a fan?"

"No, you are right. He was definitely shooting Garrett some daggers."

Gina interrupted Elizabeth. "Wait, Tony went too?"

"Yeah, why? You know it's always whoever is free from the singles group. Elizabeth and I hung out with him before and after lunch."

"Oh, that's nice," was all Gina said.

Was she jealous? Tony and Gina dated and hit it off pretty well, back when Christian had feelings for Gina but was afraid to date his brother's widow. Luckily, the two finally realized they were destined to be together. God told Gina she was supposed to be with Christian and not Tony. Tony took it hard, but they still ran into each other as they existed in many of the same circles. This town just wasn't that big.

"Anyway," continued Elizabeth. "It's like Tony was jealous or something."

"He can start pumping iron if he wants," said Anna, and everyone burst out laughing. Except Gina.

"Anna, that's not what I meant," said Elizabeth, "though that is hysterical. I actually thought maybe he was jealous of you and Garrett."

"You think Tony likes Anna?" asked Gina in surprise.

"I don't know. I'm just saying his eyes never left them during lunch."

"Wow, Anna, maybe you have two guys to choose from. When it rains, it pours," said Grace.

"Stop it. Tony doesn't like me. Hey, you know I'm not the only girl here who dates. Let's talk about Grace and Elizabeth."

The banter continued back and forth, with Grace

telling of an epically horrible first date the night before. The guy had the nerve to ask her age and said he wanted to date younger women. Gina seemed not to be listening to any of it. What was with her?

"Listen, this has been fun, but I have to get home and get to bed."

"Nope," said Anna. "Check your phone."

Gina looked down and saw a text from Christian. "I think Anna's idea is amazing. Go to bed there and sleep as long as you want. I can go to work when you get back. Love you, babe!"

"So, Anna, maybe you don't have a boyfriend because they don't like how you meddle."

"Ouch," said Grace.

"I don't care, Gina. Be mad at me. We worry about you, and Christian thought it was an amazing idea. The guest room is all ready for you. If you're nice to me, I may even have coffee and breakfast waiting for you when you get up. You deserve to indulge in some pampering."

Anna knew Gina wanted to argue, but the promise of sleep won out.

"Fine. Make me bacon?"

"That's my girl. Have a fantastic sleep."

Chapter 3

Gina walked into her house the next morning, feeling rejuvenated and ready to face the day.

"Hey, babe. So, tell me, how many hours did you get?"

Gina held up nine fingers while flashing her signature smile showing off her flawlessly straight teeth.

"Nice," he said, walking over and pulling her in for a tender kiss.

"Thanks, Chris, for letting me stay there. I was pretty peeved at Anna for butting in, but she was right. Just don't tell her I said that."

Christian let out one of his full belly laughs and set a cup of steaming coffee in front of her. She glanced in the living room and saw Eva looking like a little doll, head tilted to the side, and fast asleep in her swing.

"Where's AJ?"

"Still sleeping."

"Wow."

"I know. They went easy on me."

"Are you off to work now?"

"Are you kidding me? I have both kids sleeping and my beautiful wife in front of me. We can enjoy some uninterrupted conversation. I'm not leaving."

Gina laughed and took a sip of her dark roast coffee

with just a hint of cream.

"Tell me, what's new with the girls?"

"Well, your sister harbors a crush on a hot guy in the band at church."

"Really?"

"Crud. Don't tell her I said that. She will kill me. Though, on the other hand, I think she told your mother about him."

He raised her eyebrows. "Wow, I bet she regrets that decision."

Gina laughed again.

"Actually, Elizabeth said something I found a little odd."

"Yeah, what's that?"

"Well, when they all went to lunch after church last week, Tony was there. Elizabeth thought he seemed jealous of Anna's interest in the band hottie—sorry, Garrett."

"Why is that weird?"

"I don't know. Did you ever think Tony was interested in your sister?"

"I never gave it any thought. You and Tony dated back when I was an idiot, so let's be honest, G; I don't like to think of the fact that he kissed my wife."

She rolled her eyes at him.

"Why do you even care?"

"I don't."

"You better not." He got up from his chair, tugged her up, and took her in his arms. "The kids are still sleeping, you know. Let's not talk about ex-boyfriends anymore." Then he pulled her in for another kiss, this being one she felt down to her bones.

~

Anna walked into the church and scanned the crowd for Elizabeth, but her eyes fell on Tony first. When she made it over to their seats, Tony stood up, drew her into a hug, then gestured to the space between him and Elizabeth. Her friend leaned over and whispered in her ear. "Garrett looks extra fine today."

"What are you, twelve?" teased Anna, though Elizabeth was not wrong. She gazed at him on the stage in his light pink shirt and tight jeans, and a smile overtook her. Not many guys can pull off that color, but Garrett did it with ease. His piercing brown eyes caught hers, and he gave her a wink.

"Umm, did you see that?"

"Yes. And I'm kind of dying."

Tony said nothing.

~

Every Sunday after the last service, those part of the young singles group hung around to find whoever was free for lunch. Today it was just Elizabeth, Garrett, Anna, and Tony.

"Where do you all want to eat today?" Tony asked.

Garrett moved over to Anna with a possessive air. "Would you guys mind if Anna and I grabbed lunch together today? I've been so swamped this week that I haven't asked her out on a date."

Tony noticed Anna's smile extended to her ears.

"Sure, that's fine. Have fun. Elizabeth, you up for lunch with me?"

"Sure, enjoy, you two."

When they moved out of earshot, Tony started in.

"That guy has a lot of nerve."

"What's with you?"

"He doesn't ask her out all week, and then he just presumes she would go with him today?"

"She did go with him."

"Well, don't you think he was a little rude?"

"No, I think the guy likes her. He saw an opportunity to get to know her better and took it."

Elizabeth stopped walking, though they hadn't reached her car yet. "I'm right, aren't I? You like her?"

"What? No. I would act the same way with you!"

"Okay."

"What?"

"Nothing. Just keep telling yourself that."

~

Garrett pulled out Anna's chair for her at the brunch spot they chose. It felt juvenile, but she almost had to pinch herself to ensure this was real. She was alone with a guy she had been admiring from afar for weeks now. A handsome one who possessed a love for the Lord that was on display for all to see.

"Thanks for coming with me today, Anna. I'm sorry I haven't asked you out on a proper date yet."

"No worries. I'm glad we get to spend some time together today. Tell me, how do you like singing and playing in the church band?"

"I enjoy it. It's been a few months now, and I love it there. How long have you attended the church?"

"A few years. My sister-in-law Gina and her husband Christian—my brother—go there. But they haven't been there since you started. They have a three-year-old and just welcomed a baby girl, and it's been a little rough. They watch it online now until Eva gets on more of a schedule."

He neglected to respond as the waitress came to

19

take their drink orders and ask if they were opting for the buffet, a feast they both looked forward to indulging in.

"Shall we?" asked Garrett as he pulled out Anna's chair. It felt like forever until she rose from her seat though it was probably just a few seconds. Those penetrating eyes of his drew her in like a magnet each time she looked at him. She followed behind him, realizing how tall he was. He stood at over six feet, and though she was 5'7", he seemed almost giant-like. It intimidated her slightly, and she wondered if that was a bad thing. But he flashed her that brilliant smile of his, and the thought left as quickly as it arrived.

When they sat down with their food, the conversation stayed casual as they ate their pancakes, eggs, and everything the buffet offered. Garrett's plate was piled high, and he spent a few minutes telling her how important it was to carb-load due to his fierce workout regimen. She listened as he talked about squats, deadlifts, and bench press weights with ease.

"So, Anna, do you like to work out?" As he said it, she swore his gaze lingered over her a little too long. Was it admiration or judgment? Did she need to lose a few pounds? Was he trying to figure out if she possessed any six-pack abs under her shirt? There was no way to compete with his physique. She pushed those negative thoughts away and tried not to think about how unlike her they were.

"I love to paddleboard. Although with this crazy heat, I have to get out early or later at night, so the temperature dies down a little. It's unbearable lately."

"I know. If it weren't so hot, I would suggest we walk around a little bit after we eat."

"That's okay. I have to get back soon anyway. I head to my mom's every Sunday. All the family gets together, and I have a few things to finish before I go over there."

"You're close with your family then?" he asked while shoveling another bite of pancake loaded with syrup into his mouth.

"Extremely. They drive me crazy sometimes, but I don't know what I would do without them. God blessed me with a wonderful family. What about you?"

"I have two brothers and a sister, but they all live in Pennsylvania, where my parents are. I always loved the warm weather, and that's how I chose to go to college here and ended up staying. I can't imagine ever leaving."

"Are you close with your family?"

"I am. But it sounds like we aren't as tight-knit as yours. It's hard to stay connected all the time when you live apart."

"I can't even imagine. I'm so lucky to have my family here to support me. They are amazing. I want that for myself someday too."

Great, let's scare him away on the first date. Either he ignored it, or it didn't faze him.

"You said you work for the local newspaper as a journalist? Do you like it?"

"I love it, even though the pay stinks. I live for chasing down a lead or telling people's stories, learning about others' struggles. I can't imagine doing anything else."

"That's awesome. I don't enjoy my job in finance as much as you love your job. The work is mundane, you know. I'm good at it, but it doesn't light my fire as much as I had hoped starting out. But at least I have my singing at the church and my competitions. That's what fuels me."

"I get it, and at least you find time for other things that bring you joy. You must stay really busy."

"I do. That's why I grabbed this opportunity to take you to brunch. I hope I didn't offend your friends."

"Not at all."

"Are you sure? Tony seemed a little peeved. I get the feeling he doesn't like me all that much."

Anna got that impression, too, but kept it to herself. She had no idea what Tony's problem was with Garrett. Tony was the guy that everyone wanted to be around. She had known him since high school, and she couldn't think of a single person he didn't like—until now.

"No, Tony is a great guy. I'm sure he is fine."

"You two are close?"

"It's kind of a long story. He used to date my sister-in-law, and before that, he was good friends with her husband—my brother Christian."

"Sounds complicated."

"Maybe a little. Tony, Elizabeth, and I started hanging out more, as we love to go to the singles group together. We all have become good friends. Elizabeth is best friends with Gina, and that's how we were introduced many years ago." Her mind wandered to when they all stood as bridesmaids in Gina's wedding to her brother Alex. The love in the air that day could have filled ten thousand balloons.

"Are you okay?"

"I'm fine. We suffered a family tragedy several years ago, and it still hits me hard sometimes."

"I'm sorry if I upset you. Want to talk about it?"

"Not today, if you don't mind."

"Of course not."

He steered the conversation back to Tony, which she found odd. What was it with all these guys jealous of each other?

"Does Tony still see your brother and his wife?"

"Not recently. As I said, Gina and Christian haven't gone back to church yet since the baby came. But you know, it is a small, tight-knit community around here. Everyone runs into each other sooner or later." It's not a surprise when you live in a town with a population of around 25,000.

"Well, I'm glad you and I are getting to know each other, Anna." He pulled her chair out, and a shiver ran through her when he touched her lightly on the back. Why does that always happen? It was a rhetorical question as she knew the answer.

"Me too."

They walked to their cars, conveniently parked next to each other, and he turned and placed a gentle kiss on her cheek. Though his lips barely grazed her skin, the warmth lingered.

"This was nice. Can I call you this week?"

"Yes," was all she uttered as a reply, and he smiled knowingly at her. Did he sense how hard she was falling for him? Get it together, Anna!

"Have a great time with your family today."

She waved goodbye, and a few minutes passed until she realized she still leaned dreamily against the car with an upturned mouth that seemed to reach the moon.

Anna walked into her mother's house with full

intentions to say her hellos, then drag Gina off to a corner to spill everything about Garrett. After an endless amount of boring dates, she was eager to tell Gina about this one. Anna bounded into the room with her usual exuberance and exchanged greetings with her mom and dad, Christian, and the kids.

"Where's Gina?"

"She was beat, so I let her stay home and rest."

Anna chewed on her lips that were turned down slightly in a frown and avoided eye contact. She didn't want to show her disappointment. Too late.

"I'm sorry, sis. I know she misses you too. Things will get better when Eva gets on more of a schedule."

"I know. I just miss her so much, and Gina loves Sunday dinners. She really must be exhausted for her not to come. Are you sure she is okay, Chris?"

Helena and John shared a glance that Christian likely saw but chose to ignore. Anna shot her mother a look, signifying they would be talking about this in private after dinner.

"My mom is sad," said AJ, as he wandered over to Anna and put his arms up.

Christian gave her the death stare, and she knew he was angry with her for bringing this up around AJ. She forgot how perceptive kids are. They could catch an eye roll or a slight flare of annoyance from any angle.

"She's not sad, buddy. She probably looks that way, but that's what happens when you are tired. That's why it's so important for everyone to get enough sleep each night."

"Eva doesn't get enough sleep."

"I know, and that's why your mom is so tired. She gets up with Eva several times a night."

"Why?"

"Because babies need to eat a lot so they can grow and get strong. But in a few months, they sleep more, and your mom will be back to normal and have all this energy to run around with you."

"Thanks, Aunt Anna. I love you."

"I love you too."

She didn't have to turn toward Christian to know he was holding back tears. She knew he missed the vibrant Gina whose laugh ignited smiles in others and whose personality drew everyone into her orbit.

While her dad and Christian took AJ outside to burn off some energy and toss a ball around, Anna and her Mom settled back at the dining room table. Her mother held Eva while she slept, and Anna gazed at the baby's tiny fingers and toes, her Meditteranean skin, and the little tufts of black hair starting to grow in. Her heart swelled at the prospect of having her own infant to hold one day.

"So, when's the last time you saw Gina?" she asked her mother.

"I was just there yesterday. Stop worrying, Anna. Your brother doesn't like it when we keep pushing. He is likely concerned enough about her without us making it worse."

"Mom! Didn't I say the same thing to you the other day? We really are a pair."

"When I go over, it's to help her with the kids and around the house. It's when I leave that it's hard for her, I imagine."

"I can't believe you are telling me not to worry. Usually, I'm begging you to butt out."

Her mother laughed, half nodding in agreement.

"But, seriously, Mom, I'm even jealous of you. You get to spend time with her. I want my sister back."

"Anna, have you made a point to go see her alone? To help with the kids? I know you want Gina to listen to you talk about your church boy but what she needs right now is help."

"Wow, make me sound more selfish, why don't you?"

Her mother made no moves to fill the gaping silence echoing through the room.

"Fine, you are right. Just because Gina has healed from everything that happened, I know she still struggles—especially now when she is so hormonal."

"There's my girl."

"And by the way, church boy?"

Her mother laughed. "Yeah, just a little nickname your father and I use. I promise not to call him that when I meet him."

"We went on one date!"

"And I'm dying for you to tell me about it. Honey, I know you looked sad when you came in here today and didn't see Gina. You just need to give her a little time and space right now. You can tell me all the juicy details if you want."

"There are no juicy details ... But I like him."

"Shocker!" Then they both erupted in silly laughter, which caused Eva to wake from her nap.

"I don't want to give this precious girl up, but do you want to hold her, Anna?"

"I do, but first, let me text Gina, asking when she needs me to come over to help. You know what—I will cook for her too. Do you know if there is something she wants that she hasn't enjoyed in a while?"

"I think as long as she doesn't have to make it, anything works."

"Good point."

Anna peeked out the window to make sure the boys remained outside. "So, how is Christian doing through all this? It must be hard for him."

"It is. I think you need to make a point to spend time with your brother too. They both need a break. Maybe one day you can go over there and walk around the block with him and push the kids in their stroller."

Anna nodded in agreement and chastised herself for her selfishness and not realizing how much Christian and Gina needed support.

"And what about, Tony? You should tell him to take your brother out sometime. Those two used to be so close."

"They still are. I know Tony has tried, but I think Christian is afraid to leave Gina. But if I am there to help her, then Christian can relax too. How did you get so good at this?"

"A lot of practice."

"Christian is going to be okay, too, right?"

"Of course. You know how much he loves Gina. He simply worries about her—she and the kids are his world."

She sighed wistfully, wondering when someone would feel that way about her. Someone whose next breath depended on letting her know how much she was treasured. And Anna had an inkling Helena wasn't sure it was church boy.

Chapter 4

Anna was glad her mother spelled out precisely what Gina needed, as it turned out she was right. Gina seemed excited that Anna was coming over to spend the day with her. She was thankful for her Flex Friday schedule, allowing her to log out of work and enjoy the weekend. Anna opened the car door and started taking out the Italian food to put in the oven later for dinner. Before she knocked, AJ opened the door for her.

"Aunt Anna!"

"Hey, AJ, did your mom tell you to open the door for me?"

He nodded his head vigorously in agreement. "I was waiting at the window for you."

Gina rounded the corner, looking frazzled yet still like herself, and it immediately gave Anna comfort.

"Hey, Anna, let me help you with all that. Wow, what did you bring?"

"Your favorites, of course, and Mom tells me the best part is that you don't have to cook it."

"She knows me so well. Thank you so much for doing this. I've looked forward to it all week."

"Me too. Where's Eva?"

"I just put her down, and now it's time for this little guy to take a nap too."

"No, I want to stay with Aunt Anna."

"Don't worry, buddy. You take a nap, and I will be here when you get up."

Gina took his hand, "Guess what? She is staying for dinner too."

That put a giant grin on his face, and he followed his mother up the stairs. When Gina came down about ten minutes later, she found Anna had picked up all the blocks strewn across the floor. His latest obsession was constructing tall towers then knocking them down, but he hadn't yet grasped the importance of picking up all the pieces.

"Wow, I need to invite you over more often."

What was wrong with her? Gina shouldn't have to invite her over. She just had a baby, for goodness sake. The guilt that plagued her since that talk with her mother intensified in her gut once more.

"I can do this every Friday if you want. I'm sorry I didn't suggest it earlier."

"Stop, Anna, it's fine," she said and then gestured to the couch. "I don't know how much time we have before a kid starts crying or interrupts us. I desperately need some adult talk."

Anna immediately felt at ease, and although she missed Gina, suddenly she didn't know where to start.

"What do you want to know?"

Gina swatted her playfully on the arm. "I want to learn all about church boy."

"Our mother is a piece of work."

"You know she can't keep a secret. Though I have to say she was short on details."

"There isn't that much to tell, but I like him, Gina."

"What do you like about him?"

Gosh, how she missed her friend, and the smile

29

immediately swept up her cheeks.

"Well, I'm not going to lie. He's hot." Gina rolled her eyes, but her expression begged Anna to continue.

"I guess that's what drew me to him at first. And watching him sing on stage, he seems so devoted to God, and that pulled me toward him as well."

"That's awesome, Anna. It's so important to be with someone who shares your beliefs."

"I know, though now that I think about it, we haven't talked about our faith really, but it's nice to know that he won't be trying to push me into bed with him."

Gina raised her eyebrows. "Not necessarily."

"Yeah, I get it. I know some people say they are Christians but act differently, but I have a good feeling about him."

"What else do you have in common besides belonging to the same church group?"

"He's really into fitness—way more than me. But he is easy to talk to. And every time I see him, I get those butterflies, you know."

"Oh, I know," Gina said with a smile. "Butterflies are the best."

"It's still really early—we've only gone on one date, but we text a lot, and he calls me sometimes. I'm excited to see where it goes."

"I'm happy for you, Anna. Maybe you can invite him to a Sunday dinner?"

"Not anytime soon. But if I do, you have to come."

"Of course. And Chris told me you were upset I wasn't there."

"Stop, you don't have to explain. I need to be more understanding. You have a lot going on. I'll try to be a better friend."

"Are you kidding? You're the best friend and sister ever."

"Thanks for saying that, even though you're a liar." Before they moved on to the next topic, Eva's cries sounded through the monitor.

"Would you let me go get her?"

"Let you? Ha, be my guest."

Anna walked up the stairs and was so grateful her mother clued her into what Gina needed. She would have to thank her for that later. After changing Eva, Anna carried her downstairs and saw Gina coming back with her bottle.

"Want me to take her back?"

"No way, and if you need to go do something, don't worry about me."

She barely finished her sentence before Gina took off up the stairs, yelling behind her about badly needing a shower.

~

When Christian walked in the door at six, Anna observed her suit-clad brother as he took in the scene around him. Gina relaxed at the table, sipping a cup of tea, looking radiant in her black, slim jeans and a simple red top. And her smile went on for days, which triggered the same reaction on her brother's face. AJ was parked on the couch mesmerized by Pocoyo playing on the TV, and Eva bounced happily in her seat next to Gina.

"Hey, love, how was your day?" he asked while bending down to kiss his wife.

"Well, as you can see, I'm pretty content. Your sister has things running smoothly."

Anna laughed. "Please, you should have seen it an hour ago. AJ was running around the house making all kinds of noise, which made Eva cranky, and I was trying to get dinner ready."

"It was chaotic? Wow, that never happens when I'm home."

They both laughed, and Anna threw a dishtowel at Christian.

"Listen, you two, go gather the troops. Dinner is almost ready."

After Gina settled Eva in the swing next to her, they all piled their plates high with the eggplant parmesan, garlic bread, and salad that Anna prepared.

"Sis, this is delicious. But next time you come over, can you make my favorite dish?" he teased while Gina sent him a loving glare.

"Sure, bro, next time you pop a baby out of you, I'll get right on that. And besides, you have your mother for that. She makes you pastitsio at least once a month."

Her brother had no comeback ready for that one. Helena lived to cook her kids' favorite dishes, so Christian didn't need Anna cooking for him. Knowing that, he expertly changed the subject.

"I know you two already gabbed while I was at work. But what's the tea?"

"You're such a girl," Gina teased.

"Your sister told me all about Garrett."

"Oh, yeah, tell me about church boy."

"That woman!"

"I'm just teasing, sis. I heard he's a muscle head. Be careful."

"Oh, you're just jealous because you wish you had his guns."

They all laughed, and Anna failed to recall a recent time when the three of them enjoyed each other like this.

"So, what's new with Elizabeth?" Christian asked.

"What do you mean, don't you guys still see her?"

"We do, but you know how it gets around here. We don't get to catch up that often."

"She's great. We attend church together every Sunday and also during the week at our small group studies or get-togethers. And after church, we all go to lunch. Tony too. Oh, and by the way, he wants to hang out with you. I'll come help with the kids one night so you two can get some guy time."

"Thanks, sis, that would be awesome."

Anna grabbed another piece of bread, and when she caught Gina's eye, Anna swore her demeanor changed. Was it the mention of Elizabeth? Tony? Christian was oblivious and kept asking questions. All Anna wanted to do was change the subject. Eva started crying, and Gina leaped up and unbuckled the baby from her seat, all while murmuring about bath and bedtime.

"G, it's okay," said Christian. "I'll do it. Stay and hang with Anna."

Gina waved him away. "I had her to myself today. You never see her either. You two visit."

"I want a bath too, Mommy."

"Of course, AJ, come up with me, but say goodnight to Daddy and Aunt Anna."

"Night, Daddy. Night, Aunt Anna," he said while giving each of them a big hug.

"Good night, buddy. See you, Sunday."

Anna turned to her brother. "Let's tackle the cleanup, or I can do it if you need to go do something.

Really, I don't mind."

"No way, you cooked all this. We can clean and catch up."

Anna heard the water running upstairs, then turned to Christian while continuing to clear the plates and pile them in the sink.

"Did I upset her?"

"I don't know, Anna."

"Liar."

"Fine. Her feelings get hurt easily. I'm the bozo who brought up Elizabeth. I should have known that would make her sad. She just feels like everyone is moving on without her, and it gets her down sometimes."

"The same thing happened when I talked about spending time with Tony when we all got together for that girls' night."

"Really, sis? Why tell me that?"

"Gosh, now I'm the bozo. I didn't mean she likes Tony. You know that was over before it began because she couldn't stop thinking about you."

Christian smiled. "You're right. My wife is madly in love with me." Anna rolled her eyes.

"I meant the same thing happened that time. We were having a great time until Gina found out Liz and I hung out with Tony—the whole mood changed."

"As I said, Anna, it's hard. Two kids changes things, and it's easy to let things bother you."

"But she's okay?

"Yes."

"Are you guys doing alright? I could even stay and watch the kids and let you two go out."

"Not tonight, but I will take you up on that one of

these days. And yes, we are great. I'm the one person she seems to pour her heart out to, which is good."

"She loves you so much, Chris. I want what you guys have."

"Just be patient."

If there was a phrase she could obliterate from the human dialogue these days, that would be the one. She realized the whole kitchen was clean, then noticed Gina standing in the doorway. She wore a blank expression that unnerved Anna.

"Hey, Gina, are both kids sleeping?"

"For now."

"Well, let me get out of your hair so you two can enjoy some time together. But I told Christian I want to babysit so you guys can have a date night."

"That would be great, Anna. Thanks so much for everything today."

"Of course. It's what friends and sisters are for. See you both on Sunday."

Christian shut the door, and locked it for the night, then reached out to pull his wife in for a hug, and she immediately wiggled out of his embrace. "What the heck? 'See you both Sunday?' Your sister isn't very subtle, Chris."

Before he replied, she kept going. "I heard you guys talking about my jealousy."

He stood in silence then tried to lighten the mood. "Did you also hear the part where I am madly in love with you?"

That got her, and the smile quickly spread, and she inched closer to her husband and stroked his black hair with her thumb.

"I heard. It's why I can't be mad at you."

"Are you mad at Anna?"

"You know I'm not. I can feel when these emotions take over me, and I want to stop them, but I don't know how."

"Babe, I know you don't want to hear it, but you have to remember it's not your fault. It's the stress and the lack of sleep. Just like you have healed from everything else in your life, you will heal from this."

"I'm going to stop you right there before you start talking about my hormones. That's where I draw the line."

"Okay, how about we talk about my hormones?" He laughed, grabbed her other hand, and led her up the stairs.

Chapter 5

Tony walked to his Toyota Tacoma parked at the Home Depot near his house and caught a glimpse of Garrett leaving Chili's with a girl. The restaurant was in the next lot over, as they were both part of the Tarpon Shopping Center. Tony looked again, and there was no mistaking it was Garrett. The guy's stature wasn't exactly conducive to blending in. The woman was attractive but not nearly as mesmerizing as Anna—the girl Garrett was supposed to be dating. So why was he out with someone else? Tony climbed into his truck and called Anna right away. "Hey, want to grab a cup of coffee tonight?"

"No thanks, Garrett is stopping by in a bit."

"I just saw him out with a girl, Anna. They walked out of Chili's."

"Yeah, it's his sister. What's your problem with him? Stop acting like my big brother. I already have one of those. Quit worrying about me."

"Before I do, is it a good idea for a guy you had one date with come to your house?"

"I'm 27 years old! Are you kidding me? And do you have no faith in me, Tony?"

"I'm sorry. I don't know why I said that."

"It's fine."

"No, it's not. I'm really sorry."

"Night, Tony," she said, then hung up.

~

Anna scrutinized her appearance one more time in the mirror before Garrett arrived. Her dark hair fell loosely on her shoulders, and today it was a cross between curly and straight—she wished it decided, but every day it had a mind of its own. She didn't take the time to straighten it after her chaotic day at work. Before she obsessed any longer about her appearance, which included wondering if wearing eyeshadow was too much for a night in, she heard a knock at the door.

"Hey, Garrett, how was dinner with your sister?"

"Great, we went to Chili's."

"I know. Tony called me."

His face showed disdain and confusion, all rolled into one, with perhaps the former winning the battle. "Apparently, he thought you were on a date and wanted to warn me."

"Is there something going on between you two? Because I like you, Anna, but I don't want to get in the middle of anything."

"There's not. I don't know why he is acting this like this."

"Seriously?"

"What?

"Are girls truly that clueless sometimes?"

"Hey!"

"Sorry, but a guy only acts like that when he likes a girl."

There was that insinuation again. What was wrong with people? Why is it impossible to comprehend that members of the opposite sex could be friends?

"Tony and I are just friends." She attempted to say

it as firmly as possible but wasn't positive she succeeded.

"Just to be sure, I need to keep an eye on him from now on."

Well, there was her answer.

"Forget I said anything. Come on, sit down and tell me about your dinner."

"It was fine. As I said, my sister was in town for work, but I wish she lived closer. You know, when we talked the other night about family, and I see how tight you are with yours, it made me miss them."

"It's never too late to reach out and fix things."

"I know, and I'm definitely going to do that. You are a good influence on me, Anna."

She felt the heat on her cheeks, and from the way Garrett looked at her, it must have left a mark. Why did she turn into a bowl of jello around him? It was hard not to, with the sleeves hugging his firm muscles and his thick black hair calling to her. She wondered if it was as soft as it looked. What the heck was wrong with her? She looked down to see him holding her hand. When did that happen? When she was staring at his chest that was bulging out of his t-shirt?

"It's getting late," she said nervously. "Want to start watching the movie? I know you need your beauty sleep."

"Are you making fun of me?" he replied with a glint in his eyes.

"Maybe a little. You always tell me how sleep is important. I needed to tease you about it."

"I don't mind. When a girl teases a guy, it means she likes him, right?"

The butterflies took flight in earnest again. "You

wish."

"She shows a sarcastic side. I like it."

"Come on, let's watch the action flick we chose before your head explodes."

He laughed and nudged slightly closer, and she thought how the next hour and a half like this would be heaven.

~

Anna grabbed her keys, excited to head to Grace's for tonight's get-together. She couldn't wait to tell her friends about her date last night. She knew she beamed every time she thought of Garrett.

She knocked on the door, and Grace greeted her and then pulled her in for a tight embrace. She spotted Elizabeth already seated comfortably on the couch, relaxed and ready for their gabfest. She noticed Gina hadn't arrived yet.

"Hey, Anna, don't mind me for not getting up. I'm so cozy over here already."

Anna laughed. "No problem. The seat next to you is calling my name."

Grace brought an assortment of food and set it all down on the coffee table. Anna perused the selection of appetizers then her eyes darted to dessert. She grabbed a chocolate chip cookie. "Mmmm, Grace, these are still warm. It's official. You must host every girl's night from now on."

"Fine by me, you know I love entertaining and cooking. I wish I knew more people to do it for."

None of the girls responded, and the awkwardness settled in the air like an uninvited guest.

"Oh stop, no one needs to feel sorry for me. I'm just saying. God has a plan in mind for me; I know it. Until then, I get to fatten up you girls."

"Well, I don't like the fatten part, but I love your food," said Elizabeth. She fixed a plate filled with a cookie, homemade spinach dip, bread, and a Brie Grace baked in the oven topped with maple syrup and pecans. "Grace, this Brie is amazing."

"Why, thank you."

"What time is Gina getting here?" Liz asked.

"She just texted that she can't make it."

The disappointment descended on Anna like an impending storm. She promised to be more understanding about things like this. She knew Gina was still adjusting to the new baby, even though Eva was almost three months old now.

"I know that look, Anna," said Grace. "We all miss her but come sit and tell us all about your date with Garrett."

"Yeah, we promise to ooh and ahh in all the right places," teased Elizabeth.

"Well, before I get to that, which was amazing, wait until I tell you about Tony."

Grace and Elizabeth exchanged knowing glances. "What, you already know?"

"He called me after he talked to you. He felt so bad about it," Liz answered. "Are you willing to admit yet that the guy has feelings for you?"

"I'm not. So can I tell you about Garrett, or what?"

Chapter 6

Tony sat at the desk in his classroom, staring at his phone, willing a text to come through, all while his 10th grade English students took a test. He apologized to Anna again a few hours ago but no reply. She told him she is constantly on top of her messages at work, as sources often text or call about stories.

He looked up to find the last student standing in front of him with his paper to hand in. How long had he been there? He took it, then realized it was time for them to get to their next class. "Alright, if everyone handed in their tests, then get out of here. See you tomorrow and stay out of trouble."

"You know it, coach," said a member of the baseball team. "See you at practice."

"Don't be late," Tony called after him. Hopefully, coaching would get his mind off Anna—and Garrett—and imagining the two of them together. Maybe he would run a few sprints with the boys to work out some of his stress. He was thankful God brought him to his alma mater that had a teaching position open, and a need for a baseball coach. God always paved the way for him, and he was so grateful. But then his mind drifted to Anna again, and Tony realized students from his next class filed in. He really needed to get this girl out of his head where she occupied all of the space there. The trouble was she wasn't just any girl.

~

Tony walked off the field with one of his players and realized sweat was dripping from his forehead. That fact did not go unnoticed from his star pitcher, a senior likely headed to a division 1 college on a full scholarship.

"What's with you, coach? You never work that hard with us?" Brandon asked.

"Just wanted to see if I could keep up with you young dudes. It turns out I still got it."

Brandon rolled his eyes, then looked over at one of his teammates in Tony's English class. "So, coach, Dean said you were distracted today. Do you have girl troubles? Maybe I can give you some tips."

"You wish," he answered, giving him a friendly push. "I'm doing fine with the ladies, thanks very much. Now get out of here, and finish cleaning up the equipment."

"Alright, just remember I'm here if you need me," he said with a sly smile.

What had his life come to, that he was now getting relationship advice from 17-year-old boys? Suddenly, he felt the urge to run a few more laps.

~

Anna looked down at her phone for what felt like the millionth time that day. She kept rewriting a text to Tony but still hadn't sent anything. She erased the latest draft once again, then typed, "It's all good. Save me a seat at church Sunday," and hit send. The reply came back immediately, "You know it," followed by a big smiley face emoji, and Anna was suddenly smiling too. Her mother emerged from the kitchen with a hot cup of tea and a container of homemade almond cookies. "Who put that huge grin on your face? Church boy, I presume?"

"Maybe," she answered slyly while grabbing two cookies from the container. There was no need to let on that it wasn't Garrett. The last thing she needed was her mother to bug her about Tony too.

"So, tell me the latest about Garrett."

"I'm impressed. Thanks for using his real name, Mom."

"Don't get used to it," she joked while taking a cookie of her own. "So, what's the scoop?"

"There isn't much to tell. He came over the other night, and we watched a movie," to which her mother raised her eyebrows. "Don't! How old am I?"

Helena ignored her and continued with the questions. "When will you see him again?"

"We're going paddleboarding Saturday morning before it gets too hot."

"That's nice. I know how much you love that."

"Yeah, and surprisingly he has never done it before, so it will be fun to show him the ropes."

"And your new bathing suit?"

"Stop! You are impossible."

"Good thing you love me anyway."

"Listen, I better get going. I need to run some errands."

"Okay, have fun on Saturday. I look forward to hearing all the details in person on Sunday at dinner. Or bring him with you, and he can tell me about it himself."

"Nice try. I told you that isn't happening for a while!"

"We'll see."

Anna kissed her mother on the cheek, then said goodbye, but now all she thought about was the fact that she would be seeing Garrett while wearing a bathing suit. Hopefully, she could live up to his standards—the guy was a fitness phenom. Now she wished she never ate that second cookie.

~

Anna and Garrett headed toward the water to launch their paddleboards, her own and his rented one, and she felt more insecure than ever. She could not find an ounce of fat on him, and instinctively she sucked her stomach in. Though she knew if her friends were here, they would say, "What stomach?" They always told her how fit she was, partly because she stayed active paddleboarding and running regularly. She couldn't remember a time she lacked confidence like this but decided not to dwell on it.

"You first," Garrett said with a smile. "You are the expert here. I'm still afraid I won't be able to stay up on this thing due to my size."

"You'll be fine," she said while guiding her board in the water and gesturing for him to do the same.

"Start like this on your knees until we get out a little farther, then try standing up."

While they paddled out, she basked in the beauty of her surroundings, including the white sandy beach. She was lucky to live a mere ten-minute drive to Howard Park, where she could enjoy the water whenever she wanted. The park boasts a one-mile causeway that offers access to the Gulf of Mexico, and she never tired of the peace that enveloped her here. She said a quick prayer of thanks to God for allowing her to live in such a beautiful place.

"Alright, watch me," she said to Garrett. "And try to find your balance."

"You keeping saying the word try," he said with a gleam, yet determination, in his eye.

"Sorry—when you stand up."

She watched him intently and immediately knew this was one focused man. She guessed he wouldn't be happy if success didn't happen on the first attempt. Thankfully, he did it with ease and started paddling toward her.

"Nice job," she said, and he shot her one of those fantastic smiles that she imagined broke a lot of women's hearts.

"Thanks. So how far out are we going today? What's our plan?"

"You're pretty focused, aren't you?"

"Gotta be that way when you're a competitor."

"But we're not competing now."

He raised an eyebrow at her and paddled faster.

"Oh no, you don't. This is my domain. You will not beat me out here on the water." Then she passed him and winked.

"Well, well. I thought it wasn't a race."

"Hey, you started it. But seriously, let's just enjoy this beautiful day. How about we head toward that bank of palm trees up ahead? You think you can go that far?" she asked with a gleam in her eye.

"Oh, you are in so much trouble."

Anna sped up, thinking she would follow this man just about anywhere.

~

Two hours later, they arrived back at the launch

area with a fresh coat of brown on their skin. "What did you think, Garrett?

"I admit it is harder than it looks. That was a good arm workout. And as a bonus, I got to spend the day with a beautiful girl."

Anna turned her head down shyly and changed the subject, which often happened when given a compliment. "It's not just the arms. It's also good for strengthening the legs and your core. It doesn't feel that way, but you may notice it later."

"You love it out here, don't you?"

"It's one of my favorite hobbies when I have the time. I get grumpy if I can't get out at least once a week."

"Well, I would love to go with you again. I am pleasantly surprised at how much I like it though I'm sure the company was a huge part of it." She avoided looking him squarely in the eye again when he said it.

"I have a surprise for you if you're up for it."

"Of course."

"You don't know what it is yet."

"Doesn't matter. I'm pretty easy-going and love surprises."

"Good to know. But don't get your hopes up too much. It's just a lunch I packed for us. Want to head over to the beach area and enjoy it?"

"Yes, that was so nice of you. And I'm starving."

"Great, I brought a bunch of choices as I wasn't sure what you liked."

"Well, good news for you, I eat pretty much anything, she said while rubbing her stomach."

His eyes roamed over her, and there was that hint of self-consciousness again, but she brushed it off.

Hazards of dating a bodybuilder, she guessed.

~

About ten minutes later, they relaxed on a large blanket on the beach with a spread of cheese, meat, crackers, fruit, and veggies in front of them. Anna was impressed and was giggling like a schoolgirl inside. She hoped that wasn't evident to Garrett.

"Go ahead, help yourself."

"Thank you so much for doing this. It all looks amazing."

"No problem. I enjoyed putting it all together. I was looking forward to our date all week."

"So was I," she admitted while biting into a wheat cracker topped with sharp cheddar. She hoped there weren't any crumbs on her cheek. She was so self-conscious around this mean. "So, are you singing during church tomorrow?"

"That's the plan. I usually only get a day off if I'm away for a competition or vacation. Why? Are you looking forward to seeing me again?" he teased. She was sure her face was brightening again and hoped the color blended in with the sun she got today.

"It's cute when I compliment you and get embarrassed."

So much for that.

"I'm not embarrassed. It's the sun."

"Liar," he said while popping a piece of pepperoni topped with cheese in his mouth.

"What do you think of this sermon series about addiction?" she asked, hoping to bond with him a little over their shared faith.

"It's fine if you have issues with that, but I'm not finding it relatable to me. I'm surprised you do—is there something you aren't telling me?" he said jokingly. "Drugs, alcohol?"

"Of course not." His response surprised her. They had already listened to three sermons on the topic. The pastor emphasized we could be addicted to anything from social media, a boyfriend or girlfriend, fitness, or even food. He was the first person she talked to who didn't love it. "The pastor made it pretty clear, though, that all of us can become addicted to anything if we put things before God."

"I guess. Want to go to lunch after church tomorrow with the group?"

"Definitely."

"Great, I look forward to going out with you again. You're really fun, Anna."

"Thanks. I enjoyed today too," she said as they packed up the items on the blanket and stacked them back in the cooler.

~

As soon as she entered, Tony saw Anna and admired her-sun kissed skin that was a beautiful contrast to her simple white dress that landed at her knees. Her eyes moved to his, and he gestured her over to where he and Elizabeth sat.

"Thanks for saving my spot."

"I never break a promise," he answered with a smile showing off his extra white teeth.

"Hey, Anna," said Elizabeth, ducking her head past Tony to see Anna better. "Love the tan!"

"Thanks, girly. I went out on the water for a few hours yesterday."

"I wanted to tell you I would love to go paddleboarding with you one day," added Tony.

"Awesome, I will text you next time I plan to go."

"Won't your boyfriend be jealous?" teased Elizabeth.

"He's not my boyfriend," she said, though she secretly hoped that wouldn't be true for much longer.

Tony must not have hid his confusion well as Anna leaned over to clarify. "Garrett went out with me yesterday," she whispered. He guessed it was so those around them wouldn't overhear.

"Cool."

"Tell us all about it," Elizabeth added.

"You are going to have to wait."

Just then, Garrett started singing, and all eyes moved to the stage as the congregation began worshipping. All eyes but Tony's.

~

"Wow, what another great sermon," said Anna when the last song ended. Elizabeth left to say hi to a friend. They all planned to meet up in the lobby to head to lunch.

"I am getting so much out of this series," said Tony.

"I said the exact same thing yesterday. It's so applicable to our daily lives."

"It's not what you typically think about when you hear the word addiction. It's basically when you put anything else before God."

"Exactly. I'm kind of sad next week is the last one."

"Me too."

"Are you headed to lunch with the crew?" asked Anna as they started to make their way out.

"No, I think I am skipping today."

"Why? You always go."

Luckily, he already had plans, as he couldn't bear to

see her and Garrett together and hear them talking about their day together. Or watch Garrett touch Anna tenderly, or worse yet, see her respond to his affection. Just thinking about it made his breath come faster. And not in a good way.

"I told my dad I would come over and help him with some jobs around the house."

"You're such a great guy."

"Whatever," he said shyly, then said goodbye before she told him he was a great friend too. Not what he wanted to hear.

Chapter 7

Anna pulled up to her parent's house and saw her brother's car already in the drive. She tried not to get her hopes up, but she prayed Gina came today.

"Hey, sweetie," said her dad as he pulled her into a giant hug, enveloping her in his strong arms.

"Hey, Dad," she said with a massive smile while leaning in to kiss him on the cheek.

"Oh, here we go," said Christian, as he rounded the corner. "Your favorite child has arrived."

"Will you stop with that!"

"Relax, Dad. I'm kidding. I only say that every time just to get a rise out of you."

"You're a real comedian, son."

"Does that make me your favorite?"

"No comment."

While Dad and Christian ribbed each other, Gina strode out of the kitchen and embraced her tightly.

"What was that for? And can I please have another one?" said Anna, as she leaned in to give Gina a squeeze of her own.

"I'm just excited to see you. Eva is sleeping, AJ is occupied with all the family doting on him, so let's go catch up before it all blows up." Gina led Anna in the kitchen, where Helena was hard at work preparing the meal. Anna didn't even bother asking to help, as her stubborn mother always refused her requests.

"Is that fish I smell?" she asked while pecking her mother on the cheek.

"Fresh mackerel, my famous roasted vegetables, and pita bread."

"Yum."

"It will be about 30 more minutes, but I have it pretty well under control. Let me come sit, and you can tell us all about your date yesterday and lunch today."

"You two are relentless."

"You just got here," said Gina. "Just wait."

"First, how was paddleboarding? Did you fall off your board cuz you couldn't keep your eyes off his pecks?"

"You know, there is more to him than his physique. Like, he sings. In church."

"So, you were attracted to his faith and his muscles?"

"Yes, Gina."

"Remember what I told you ..."

"I know! Really, did I say I missed you? You're kind of worse than my mother right now!"

"Hey, I'm offended," said Helena feigning hurt.

"Sorry, we will stop teasing you. Tell us about it."

"It was a great day. We were out on the water for about two hours. Then he surprised me by packing a lunch, and we relaxed and got to know each other for a while."

"What did you talk about?" Gina asked with sincerity in her brown eyes.

"I don't know. Nothing. Everything. Church. Fitness. Family."

"Speaking of family, when is he coming ..."

"Mom!"

"Sorry, you can't blame me for trying."

"We're just messing with you," said Gina. "At least I am. I know your mother does want him to come over so she can interrogate him," and they all laughed.

"I'm glad you had a good time. How was lunch today?" asked Helena while getting up from the table to stir the olive oil and lemon sauce for the fish that was simmering on the stove.

"It was a smaller group, but it was good. Tony didn't come, though. Something is off with him, and I can't figure out what it is."

Gina looked at Christian, who walked into the kitchen cradling Eva in his arms, and everyone stopped talking. "What? You can talk about the guy when I'm around. I didn't want him to be with Gina, but as far as I'm concerned, he can date whoever he wants— including you, sis. And I think everyone forgets he was my friend first."

"First of all, what are we, back on the playground? Second, I don't want to date Tony! I just told them all about my weekend with Garrett."

"Oh, church boy. I don't have a good feeling about him."

"You don't even know him."

"I know."

"How can you have a feeling?"

"Brother's intuition."

"You guys are impossible."

"I know how to solve this," interrupted Helena. "Invite him to dinner." She almost couldn't get the words out and keep a straight face. Anna and Gina exploded with laughter, while Christian was not far behind. Anna knew if she looked in a mirror, she would see a smile as full as the moon—that's how crazy happy she was to be here in this kitchen, surrounded by her family.

~

Before leaving for work, Anna decided she would go paddleboarding after she left the office. She remembered Tony's comment, so she picked up her phone to type. "Going PB after work. Want to come?"

Tony was already at school, talking to some of his students when he heard the text, and couldn't hide his excitement when he saw the message. He typed back, "I'm in. What time?"

"Come right after practice. Can you meet me at the dock at six so we have time before it gets dark?"

"No prob." He looked up to find two pairs of eyes, studying him with interest.

"What's up, Mr. D? Is that your girlfriend?"

"Well, look at the time; class is starting."

"We will get it out of you one of these days, you know."

"Not a chance. Besides, there's nothing to tell," he said, all the while thinking 6:00 couldn't get here fast enough.

~

Tony was surprised he arrived before Anna, which gave him time to rent his board. He turned toward the water and spotted her walking toward him, her trim figure on display in her two-piece red bathing suit. He suddenly wished he had focused a little more on developing his six-pack over the past few months. After the things he overheard from the girls talking, it seemed Anna was into that stuff, which honestly surprised him.

"Your worth is found in Me, not what others think."

He knew that—he always did. *"Lord, thank you for that message, and please help me stop being insecure around her. May your will be done."*

"How did you beat me here?" Anna said with a grin, sending a jolt of electricity right through him.

"I worked the guys extra hard, so I let them go 15 minutes early."

"Nice. Did you save some energy to keep up with me?"

"What do you think? Lead the way."

They talked incessantly on the way out, often speaking over the other, and Tony wondered if it was like this when she was with Garrett. So much for shedding those insecurities.

"How did your friend do the other day out here on the water?"

"He did great—especially for a first-timer."

"Not as good as me, though, right?"

"You guys and your macho competitiveness. I will never get it."

"Just like we will never understand you females."

She took her paddle and flung some water at him. "Well, one thing is for sure, time didn't fly by with him like it did today."

"That's because you can't get enough of my witty conversation."

He expected a smart comeback and was surprised at her response. "I do enjoy your company. Why do you think I invited you?"

For some reason, that flustered him, and he took the focus off himself. "Is Garrett not easy to talk to?"

"You know how it is when you start dating

someone. It's kind of awkward in the beginning."

"It shouldn't be."

"I just mean you are getting to know each other, and you don't want to say the wrong thing. Like when I'm with you, I can be myself and relax—and have fun."

"You don't have fun when you are with him?"

"Forget I said anything; it's hard to explain. I only meant it's so easy to be around you. In fact, why hasn't some girl snatched you up already?"

"I guess I haven't met the right girl—or if I did, she was unavailable."

"Are you still stuck on Gina?"

"No way! I was just using that as an example. She and Christian are perfect for each other. But even when we were together, it was natural to be around her. I don't think it should be hard with Garrett, Anna."

"We can't all be as perfect as Gina."

"Anna!"

"I'm sorry, I can't believe I said that. Forget it."

"You have no idea how incredible you are. God was pretty close to perfection when He made you."

Did those words really come out of his mouth? He could already see the shock in her dark eyes before she turned them down at the water. But then her humor came roaring back.

"What do you mean *close* to perfection?"

"And you are so humble." He took his paddle and shot some water her way this time, making her squeal and laugh simultaneously.

"Come on, race you back," she shouted before turning her board and picking up speed while he followed behind, trying to keep up with the long strides she made with her oar.

After saying goodbye to Tony and making plans to do this again, Anna got in her car, checked her phone, and saw five messages from Garrett—and a missed call. She put the phone back in her purse and decided to text him later when it rang.

"Anna, where have you been?"

"I was paddleboarding."

"Alone at night?"

"I was with Tony," and before she could remind him, she had been going out alone on the water for years and was a grown woman; he started in on her.

"I thought you said you two didn't have a thing."

"We don't, but he's a good friend, and you know that. Listen, I have to get home and shower. Why don't you call me later this week?" and she hung up. Men.

Chapter 8

Anna grabbed her vanilla latte from the counter then sat down at the table where Elizabeth was already sipping her coffee.

"I'm so glad you texted me to meet before work," began Elizabeth.

"Me too. I have to meet someone for an interview here at 9, and since it's close to where your office is, I was hoping it would work out. So, tell me, what's new with you? Let me live vicariously through my fabulous friend."

Elizabeth wiggled her perfectly groomed blonde eyebrow at her. "If it weren't 8 in the morning, I'd ask if you were hitting the wine."

"Very funny."

"And we all know you aren't living vicariously through me. You're the one who had dates with two guys this week."

"First of all, Tony is my friend, and second, how often do you talk? Maybe you two should get together."

"Tony is an amazing guy, but no one can compete with you in his eyes, Anna."

"He told you that?"

"No, and he would flip a lid if he knew I was saying this. But it's true. We both know how good I am at reading people, and his feelings for you are obvious. To me, anyway, but hey, I know both of you well, so maybe that's why I notice it. I'm sorry, I didn't mean to make you uncomfortable. How's Garrett?"

She told her all about his call two nights ago and that they hadn't talked since. "Please don't tell Tony that."

"I won't, Anna. You are one of my best friends. You can trust me. What are you going to do about Garrett?"

"Wait until he apologizes, of course. I like him, Liz, but I did nothing wrong here. I'm not reaching out."

"And what if he doesn't text you?"

"Then it's not meant to be."

"I'm proud of you."

"You seem surprised. Am I that pathetic when I talk about him?"

"Not at all. I just know you want to find someone special to start a family with someday. I'm impressed that you aren't settling."

"If that were the case, I would have married someone else a long time ago."

"Very true."

"Have you talked to Gina recently? We had a great time last Sunday at Mom's. But since then, we have both been busy and only talked over text messages.

"Yeah, it's kind of the same with us. Our girls' nights in are nice, but we should get her out of the house and out to dinner one night."

"That sounds awesome. Can you start a chain with all of us—and Grace, of course, and set it up?"

"On it. Listen, I have to head to work."

Anna stood up to hug her friend. "Thanks for meeting me."

60

Elizabeth gave her one last wave and flitted out the door. Her blond hair waved behind her, and the appreciative stares of more than one pair of male eyes followed her out. Anna looked at her watch and realized she had about ten minutes to spare until her interview arrived, so she scrolled through her phone when a text from Garrett popped up.

"I'm sorry for the other night. I was a jerk. Can I take you out Friday night to make up for it?"

Without hesitating, she typed, "What time?" and hit send before she could second-guess her decision.

~

Anna looked at herself in the mirror and was pleased with her appearance. Her often unruly hair cooperated nicely and laid on her shoulders in soft curls. At first, she debated her mauve lipstick, but it balanced the rest of her look, her subdued blush and eye shadow. She looked down at her burnt orange dress one last time and no longer wondered if it was too much. It fell to the knee and was strapless but not too showy. Perfect for the summer heat, she thought as the doorbell sounded.

"Wow," was all he said when she answered it.

"Come on in."

"You look beautiful, Anna."

"Thank you."

"So, where are we going?"

"Well, now I don't want to take you anywhere with you looking like that."

She figured somewhere in there was a compliment, but why did it make her slightly uncomfortable? She waited for him to make up for it, but she asked if he was ready to go when he didn't.

~

He took her to Antonio's, a popular Italian restaurant in town that everyone loved—including her parents and Christian and Gina. In fact, it's where her brother and his wife had one of their first dates.

"That color looks amazing on you, Anna," he said as they sat down and opened their menus.

"Thank you."

Despite the awkward comment at her house, she enjoyed their dinner. She forgot all about the drama from the other night until he brought it up after they finished dessert—a to-die-for tiramisu. She ate most of it as he was on a strict diet. So while she enjoyed her homemade meat ravioli with Bolognese sauce, he opted for salmon, asparagus, and brown rice.

"About the other night ..."

She cut him off. "It's okay; you already said you were sorry."

"No, I have to say this. I like you, Anna. And if we're dating, I don't want you seeing other guys."

"I'm not. Tony is my friend."

"Well, I don't want you seeing him if we're going out."

"Excuse me? I'm shocked you are acting like this. It's not like this is some random guy—it's Tony. You know what a great person he is—you hang out with him at our singles group and during lunch on Sundays."

"I don't hang out with him, Anna."

"Okay, well, you see him twice a week. You know him and that we are just friends."

"I don't want you seeing him."

"Then I guess you and I are over before we even started. Take me home, please."

~

"Girl, I am so proud of you," said Gina, as she sipped her glass of merlot, even though they were sitting at the local Taphouse and Grill that boasted an array of ale options.

"It's not like I had a choice," replied Anna, as she sipped her pale ale.

"Yeah, clearly he doesn't know how feisty you are, or he would never have said that," said Grace.

"Cheers to that," added Elizabeth, as she raised her mug so they could all clink glasses.

"Have you heard from him since then?" asked Gina.

"No, and it's fine."

They all studied her.

"Okay, I like him, but we all know no one is going to boss me around."

Elizabeth giggled, and Anna turned toward her. "Listen, you can't tell Tony any of this."

"Why would I do that? I'm offended you would even say that—especially since we have already been over this."

"Sorry."

Anna wasn't surprised when Gina jumped in. "So, just when I planned to go back to church Sunday and see 'Mr. Church Boy' in person, it's over."

"You're coming to church? Oh, I'm so excited. I call dibs on holding Eva during service," and they all laughed. "Enough about me. Gina, how are things? Getting any more sleep lately?"

"A little. Christian started to get up with her one time per night, so that helps. But then I am consumed with guilt since he has to go to work each day."

"You shouldn't," answered Grace. "Just because

you are home doesn't mean you aren't working hard and don't need your rest too. It's important for your sanity."

"God, I love you, Grace."

"Hey," said Elizabeth in mock horror.

"You know I love you too. Your turn, Liz. What's new in your life?"

"Same old, same old."

They all rolled their eyes, and Anna stepped in.

"Oh, wait until you hear this; I even forgot to tell Liz. The other day we met for coffee, and when she left, she had at least two pairs of cute male eyes on her."

"It's Liz," said Gina. "Nothing new about that. One of these days, she will snag one of those interested guys."

"Stop, you two. Okay, Grace, your turn."

Anna noticed Grace look sheepish, a look she had never witnessed on her friend before.

"My ex-husband and I are starting to talk again."

"What?" Gina exclaimed a little too loudly. "Why didn't you say anything?"

Three pairs of eyes moved to Grace and honed in on her perfect features, ones that didn't show her 58 years. Anna could only hope she would age as gracefully as her friend.

"Because it just started, and I don't know what it means. But God does, and I'm placing it all in His hands."

"Just be careful," said Gina, and Anna could tell how much Gina cared about her. Grace was there for Gina when Anna deserted her after Alex and Teresa died. As horrible it was to admit, Anna felt relief that Gina's focus was on Grace now and not the fact that

Elizabeth and Anna had coffee the other day. It was a split second, but Anna noticed the look that passed over her face when she mentioned it.

"Wait a second. I am the one old enough to be your girls' mother—not the other way around."

"It doesn't mean we don't worry about you too, Grace," said Elizabeth. Those two had become close as well. It was Grace who was at the hospital comforting Elizabeth and drying her tears when Gina was falling apart during her delivery with AJ.

"I know, girls, and I love you for it." The waiter came back then with their change.

"Clearly, we have to meet a little earlier next time," said Anna. "Who knew our lives were so exciting, and we had so much to talk about?"

Their laughter could be heard throughout the busy restaurant, and they vowed to get together again as they left.

"See you Sunday," said Anna to Elizabeth and Gina.

"Save me a seat upfront, so I can shoot daggers at church boy for you," teased Gina.

Anna left with a smile on her face and a little less anxiety about showing up on Sunday and facing Garrett.

~

Anna arrived early to save a row for her friends but stupidly realized that put her front and center to Garrett, who was singing with the band before the service started. To make it worse, she looked at the door, and the first to arrive was Tony, who hugged her immediately. Though Anna couldn't see him, she imagined Garrett shooting daggers at her, all while praising the Lord in song. Thankfully, Christian and Gina entered at that moment.

"Hey, little Eva, come to your Auntie Anna."

"Nice to see you too, sis."

She shot her brother a sarcastic look and embraced Gina, who immediately whispered in her ear. "Yikes, you were not kidding. He looks even better up close."

"I heard that, wife," joked Christian.

"Did you get AJ all settled in Sunday School?"

"Yes, he couldn't wait to play with the other kids. I need to start setting up play dates for him."

Tony walked over and embraced Christian in a bear hug.

"Bro, long time, no see," and Anna could tell how happy it made her brother at seeing his friend again.

Elizabeth arrived, spotted Tony sitting next to Anna, and immediately made him scoot over a spot. "Sorry, Tony, but I need to be near this precious baby."

Anna looked up and swore she saw a glint of satisfaction from Garrett at the new assignments.

When the service ended, Anna passed Eva back to her mother, as many people hovered around Gina to welcome her and get a glimpse of the baby.

"Are you two going to lunch today?" asked Tony.

"Not me," said Anna.

"Me either."

Anna turned to her friend. "Elizabeth, don't miss out on a time you love on my account. You and Tony should go and have fun," then she glanced at Tony, who looked utterly lost. A part of her was happy Elizabeth hadn't blabbed the news but then was immediately sorry she ever doubted her.

"What am I missing?"

"Anna stopped seeing Garrett."

"I'm sorry."

"Don't!"

"Okay, I'm not sad, but if you are, then I am sorry, Anna."

Elizabeth walked away right before Tony asked Anna what happened.

"He told me I couldn't hang out with you anymore."

Anna didn't think she would ever see Tony at a loss for words, as they were always so comfortable around each other. When he continued to be immobile, she filled the gaping silence.

"It's not a big deal," then the rest of the group joined them.

"We all decided since you aren't going to lunch today that everyone should come to my mom's later for Sunday dinner."

"I'm in," said Tony and Elizabeth simultaneously.

~

"Hey, Mom," said Anna as she entered the kitchen and greeted her with a kiss.

"What time is it?"

"Relax, it's only three."

Her mother stopped what she was doing and gestured for Anna to sit at the table.

"Lay it on me. You never come this early."

"You're exasperating; you know that."

"It's a gift."

"I just wanted to let you know I'm not seeing Garrett anymore, and I don't want to talk about it when Liz and Tony are here."

"Okay, but why? You guys tell each other everything."

"Garrett and I aren't seeing each other because he told me I had to stop hanging out with Tony."

"Wow," said her dad, who joined the conversation and grabbed a pretzel from the bowl in front of them.

"John Andros, since when do you care about these kinds of things?"

"When it's my precious daughter. Do I need to beat someone up, Anna?"

"No, Dad," she said, leaning in for a kiss. "But thanks for the offer."

"John, you interrupted. Keep going, Anna."

Anna noticed the daggers her mother shot her husband and laughed inwardly.

"That's it. Of course, I'm not going to stop being friends with him, so end of story."

"What does Tony think of all this?" asked her mother.

"I don't know. He seemed kind of shocked."

"Hmm," was all her mother said, and Anna looked knowingly at her father. They both knew Helena was thinking up a storm, and Anna hoped she wouldn't make things uncomfortable today. Who was she kidding?

~

"Mrs. Andros, dinner was delicious," said Tony, patting his stomach in delight.

"I'm glad you liked it. I will send you home with some."

"That's not necessary."

Anna leaned over and mock whispered, "Don't even try to argue."

He smiled back at her, and Anna suspected her mother was already forming new romance ideas in her head.

"Mom, I will clean up if you feed Eva her bottle for me," said Gina.

"Aren't you clever? You know that is the only way to stop me from doing the dishes."

"I'll help," said Elizabeth, while immediately gathering up the plates as Anna joined her.

"I will stay here and keep this guy company," and John gathered up AJ and slung him over his shoulder, resulting in a slew of screams and laughter.

"That leaves us men," said Christian to Tony. "Want to head to the sunroom and have a beer?"

"Sure." Christian handed him a bottle of Peroni.

"Nice," said Tony. "Are you coming around to the Italian side? Gina and I welcome you here," referring to their shared Italian roots. "Sorry, man, dumb thing to say."

"Stop it. You and Gina dated forever ago. And you and I were best buds back in the day. I don't want this to be weird."

"Me either, thanks, bro," he said, clinking bottles with him.

"How is your baseball team this season?"

"Really good. I think this could be our year."

"Wow. I will plan on catching a game or two. Anna can come with me."

He shot him a look.

"What? I'm certainly not bringing my wife. I don't want her seeing you in those tight baseball pants."

"Dude!"

"I'm kidding. Speaking of baseball, I think the Rays are playing tonight," he said, leaning over for the remote.

"Yeah, hopefully, they can shut down the Yankees."

"You wish."

"A guy can dream."

"That's exactly what you're doing if you think the Yankees are going to beat the Rays," said John, grabbing a beer and taking the spot in the oversized chair next to the couch.

"Where's everyone?" asked Christian.

"They're in the family room, and Anna just went upstairs to change Eva, and AJ followed along. I figured I would come to hang with you men."

~

Helena spoke in a voice that was a few octaves lower than her usual tone.

"Quick, before Anna comes back. What's with Tony? He likes her, doesn't he?"

Elizabeth and Gina exchanged glances.

"Oh, come on. It's obvious. How did I not know this before?"

When no one answered, she kept firing questions.

"Does Anna like him?"

Now that Helena started this line of conversation, the two girls jumped in but not before turning around once more to make sure Anna was still upstairs.

"I don't think she does, but I think she's crazy. Tony is a catch," answered Elizabeth.

"Is it because of Garrett? Maybe now that he is out of the picture, she will start to see Tony in a new light."

"What do you think, Gina?" Helena asked her.

"I'm going to check on Anna and see if she needs any help."

Elizabeth looked at Helena as what she said hit her.

"Oh my gosh, now who's oblivious?"

"It's fine, Helena, obviously Gina and Tony's relationship is history, but I think because of it, the whole situation makes her uncomfortable."

"So, if Anna and Tony got together, Gina would be okay with it?"

"What are you planning in that devious little head of yours?"

"It depends. Are you in?"

"Definitely."

"Well, let's just say you and Tony may just be a permanent part of Sunday dinners from now on."

"No complaints here."

~

When Gina walked into the guest room Helena had set up for the kids, Anna immediately bristled.

"Come to check up on me? I was about to head downstairs."

"You may want to wait."

"Why, what is my mother doing now?"

"Probably planning your wedding to Tony."

Anna burst out in a full belly laugh.

"Wow, I thought you would go marching down there and give her a piece of your mind."

"Would it help?"

"Not a bit."

"Then I would rather stay up here and hang out with you until she gets bored and comes looking for us."

"I'm game."

Chapter 9

Tony finished delivering the big pep talk to his baseball team before they headed out to the field for warm-ups. The pressure was on for them this year, and though no one mentioned it, Tony knew from all the tense expressions and furrowed brows that it was on all their minds. Last year, they were two games away from making it to the state finals, and they only lost two seniors from that impressive lineup. Two of his returning players, Brandon and Dean, were his stars, and Tony knew their only goal this year was to make it to States—and get the attention of college scouts. Add in a few new promising freshmen and a transfer student, a hotshot, yet talented outfielder, made Tony think this was their year. So, in the quiet moments before the game started, why did his thoughts turn to Anna? It had been two weeks since dinner at the Andros' house, and though he saw her at church two days ago, he still missed her. They traded some texts about paddleboarding, but with his crazy baseball schedule, it had been hard for him to get away.

Christian texted him earlier to apologize that he couldn't make it to the game but would be at a future one soon and wished him luck against their rival. It was a tough school that Tony wished wasn't on the schedule for the first match-up. But they were ready.

The umpire signified that the game was about to begin. Tony sent a silent prayer of thanks to God for allowing him to work with these great kids and serve as an example to them. He then prayed the game would go well, no one would get injured, and the team competed to the best of their abilities.

~

Three hours later, Tony was all smiles as he entered his house, thankful that he was minutes away from showering all the sweat and grime from the day. He heard his phone ding and figured it must be Christian texting him back about the win. His heart pumped faster when he discovered it was Anna.

"Chris told me about your victory today. Congrats coach. Take this team all the way."

"Thanks. So proud of them."

"They are lucky to have you."

When she said things like that, he was always at a loss. It was hard not to read into every little word, looking for the meaning he wanted to see.

"We have practice early Saturday morning. Want to go boarding after that?"

"Yes, looking forward to it. Have a great night."

He definitely would, and it had nothing to with baseball.

~

Anna still held her phone firmly in her hand when it rang. She sucked in a deep breath before answering

"Hey, Garrett."

"Anna. I'm glad you picked up. I didn't think you would."

"Then why did you call?"

"Sorry, let me start over. I was a jerk and never

73

should have told you to end a friendship that means a lot to you."

"Thank you."

"Would you be willing to give me a second chance?"

"What did you have in mind?"

"Are you up for paddleboarding after work Thursday?"

She thought of Tony's game, as she planned to go with her brother. But she never told Tony she would be there.

"Sounds fun."

"Great, I'll meet you there at six."

"Perfect."

"Thanks for being so great, Anna," then he hung up, and she wondered if she made the right decision.

~

On Thursday afternoon, her cell vibrated at her desk, and Anna welcomed the break. She was working on a complex story and needed a quick breather. "Want me to pick you up for the game today?" read her brother's text.

"I have plans; I'll catch the next one."

"Oh, sorry, I thought you said you were going."

"I wasn't sure but tell Tony I said good luck."

"Will do. See you Sunday."

~

Anna was surprised at how much fun she had with Garrett on the water earlier. The awkwardness they had last time of getting to know each other was gone, and she enjoyed their banter and friendly competitiveness. Still, she already saw herself looking forward to Saturday when she would go again—this time with

Tony. Shoot, she never asked about the game, so she grabbed her phone.

"Another win, I hope?"

"Yes, it was close, but we pulled it out and won 8 to 7."

"Awesome. I'll be at the next one. And I'm looking forward to Saturday."

"Me too."

~

This time, Anna arrived first, so she was waiting when Tony strode up in his black swim trunks and Marlins tank top. His skin looked even darker than normal—it must be all those afternoon workouts with the team.

"Hey, coach. Ready to get schooled on the water?"

"Whoa, extra feisty today, I see. Bring it on."

"Oh, it's on," and she raced him to the water's edge.

"I know why you love it out here. We are blessed to have this so close."

"That's what I think every time," she answered. "So, your next game is a tough one on Monday. You ready?"

"I'm impressed."

"Oh, come on, did you forget you and my brother were the star baseball players, and my dad dragged me to every game?"

"True. And yes, we are prepared. The team is on fire, and most importantly, it's been a while since I've seen a group come together so well."

She gave him one of those "come on now" looks.

"What?"

"Tony, they are like that because of you. I'm so glad you were given the opportunity to teach and coach these kids. I don't know of anyone who would be a better influence than you."

"Wow, Anna, thanks."

"You're welcome."

"Will you be at the game?"

"Definitely."

"I hoped to see you at the last one. But it was cool for Christian to come. You should have seen your brother soaking up all the attention from the team. They all knew his stats and his record, and I swore someone was going to whip out some paper and ask for an autograph."

"Well, I'm glad I wasn't there to see that," she joked. "I will be in the front row at the next one."

"I'm holding you to that," then he took off, and she tried to ignore the fact that she conveniently left out her reason for not attending the game.

~

Anna sat at church waiting for everyone to arrive and prayed her actions didn't blow up in her face. Why had she neglected to tell anyone she went out with Garrett again? And what would happen if he came over and asked her to go to lunch? She looked over to see Elizabeth and Tony entering. Thank goodness her brother and his family couldn't make it today as Gina's parents were visiting. They decided to stay home to watch the service. But she would have to face them later as they were all gathering at her mom's for dinner.

"Hey, Anna," said Tony. "Sorry, we were a little later than normal. I decided to pick this one up, and, shocker, Liz wasn't ready on time."

"What can I do? I always have to look my best."

"When do you ever not look amazing?" answered

Tony.

"Why, thank you, sir."

Before Anna had a chance to analyze that exchange and her reaction to it, the service started with praise and worship. She didn't think she imagined Garrett looking right at her during every song, making her middle turn to mush. When the sermon concluded and the band retook the stage, Garrett continued to stare directly at her with that smoldering look that always did her in. Then the service ended, and while the band remained for a final song while people congregated, the three of them talked about their plans for the day.

"Do you guys want to go to lunch?"

"Not me," answered Elizabeth. "I have some things to get done before we all head to your mom's for dinner. I'm so excited to see Gina's parents. Tony, you're still coming, right?"

"I don't know. Obviously, Gina is happily married, but it's awkward. I know I never met her parents when we were dating, but still."

"You're crazy. And my mom will kill you if you don't come."

"Fine, I guess I will have to suffer through another one of Helena's amazing meals. But if I'm going, I'm skipping lunch. We have a big game tomorrow, and I need to do some prep. I have to run to the restroom. Liz, I will meet you at the car."

Anna and Elizabeth stayed behind to talk for several more minutes, so she didn't notice that Garrett stopped Tony on his way out.

~

"Hey man, can I talk to you for a minute?"

"Sure," said Tony, not knowing what else to say

77

and wondering why Garrett was pulling him aside, as most of their conversations up to now were always part of a group.

"I want to apologize for telling Anna to break off her friendship with you. I know now that was wrong, and I wanted to apologize personally."

"I appreciate that man, but you should probably tell her, not me."

Garrett gave Tony a quizzical look. "I already did, didn't she tell you?"

"She didn't."

"Yeah, we are all good, and we even went out the other night. I really like her, and I won't mess this up again."

There was that ache again in his chest. Was it from Garrett's news that Anna didn't trust him, or all those emotions wrapped into one? He saw Elizabeth heading over and was thankful for the escape.

"See ya, man," was the only goodbye he could manage, as he turned, eager to get out of there.

"What's with you?" asked Elizabeth as they walked to the car. "And what was Garrett talking to you about?"

He opened the car door for her, then walked around to the driver's side, got in, and started the air conditioning but made no moves to leave.

"Did you know he and Anna went out the other night?"

"What?"

"You didn't know?"

"No. But we have both been busy. She kept saying we would catch up at dinner later. Maybe she was going to tell us."

"I went paddleboarding with her the other night, and apparently, this was after they went out. She didn't say a word."

"I'm sorry, Tony."

"I know she doesn't think of me as anything more than a friend, but then why wouldn't she tell me this?"

"Come on. I don't blame her. It's awkward. You two are good friends, and here comes this guy who tells her to stop seeing you, and then he apologizes, and she goes back to him. It's not something exactly easy to bring up in the conversation."

"I guess."

Just then, Tony saw Anna and Garrett walk out of church toward Garrett's car, and the knife twisted deep into his gut.

"Tony, if this is killing you, which it seems like it is, you need to reveal your feelings."

"I can't."

"If you don't, those two are just going to keep getting closer."

"I'm not going to beg her, Liz."

"Beg her? You are unbelievable. You haven't even told her you like her beyond friends."

"She has to know."

"Guys are unbelievable."

"Girls aren't a picnic either," then he pulled away before he had to see them a minute longer and wonder what their plans were for the day and how he was going to face her later.

He pulled up in front of Liz's house, and before she could open the door, he jumped out and opened it for her.

"Man, if this is how you treat your friends, you

must be like the most perfect boyfriend ever."

He looked at her with an air of disbelief.

"Ok, that was dumb. Gina told me that you were pretty perfect."

"And look where that got me."

"I feel like I need to go buy you a pint of ice cream," she said, which finally got a laugh out of him.

"Come on, Tony. God has the perfect woman for you out there. I don't know if it's Anna or not, but He does. You need to have faith."

"Thanks, Liz."

"No problem. How about I pick you up later for dinner?"

"Come on; I really don't want to go now."

"Tony, I'm sorry, but you have to suck it up. We are all friends here, and none of us wants that to end. You have to figure out how to be around her."

He wondered if that was even in the realm of possibility.

~

Anna admired Garrett's long, powerful stride as he walked toward her with a small white bakery box in his hand. They had spent the afternoon together at a street fair downtown, and she was a little surprised at what a great time they had. She couldn't believe this was the same man she swore she would never talk to again one week ago. But he apologized to her and Tony. She couldn't be mad at him—she just hoped Tony saw it that way. She didn't want him to find out she was out with Garrett the other night. Not that it was a secret, but she would rather not explain it—or hurt his feelings.

"Hey, babe," he said while handing her the box. "The guy said you are going to love this. I told him you have a sweet tooth and that baklava is your favorite— he said this is the best you will ever taste."

"Don't let my mother hear you say that." She took a small bite, all while dissecting the term of endearment he just used with her. Was her blush creeping all the way to her ears? She no longer cared, as the sweet, nutty filling, combined with the flaky pastry, filled her senses.

"So?"

"Well, I was about to tell you that it would be impossible for me to like it more, but this is amazing. Did you get any?"

"Nah, a guy has to watch his figure."

"I don't think I have ever heard that line before."

"Guess you never dated a body-building health nut."

"This is true."

"Speaking of dating," he said while taking her hand. "I really like you and don't want to see anyone else."

When she didn't say anything, he spoke again.

"What about you?"

"I'm not seeing anyone besides you."

"That's what I wanted to hear." Then he pulled her close, gently yet with an air of possessiveness, and asked if she would come to his house to watch a movie.

"I can't," then she looked at her watch and immediately knew her mother would kill her. "I have to go."

"What's wrong?"

"I'm late for dinner at my mom's. I have never been late."

"She will understand. Can't you skip today?"

"Never. I love hanging with everyone—my brother

and his family. And I have to be there tonight. My sister-in-law's parents are in town, and I haven't seen them in forever."

"I can come."

"No," she said more forcefully than she intended, causing him to drop his arm from around her shoulder and form a scowl. What guy wants to meet a girl's parents when they have only been on a few dates? "I'm sorry. My family is just intense—amazing—but kind of overwhelming."

His demeanor softened slightly just as she received a text.

"Is that your mom?"

"No, it's Tony, warning me that I better get there fast."

"Why is Tony there?"

"He's like family," she answered, silently chastising herself for telling him about the text. "I thought we were over this."

"I didn't know how much time you spent with him, Anna. I'm not comfortable with this."

Before she could question her decision, she typed a reply, "I'm sorry, I'm not going to make it tonight. I will text my mom now." She regretted it immediately when she recognized the note of victory in Garrett's gaze.

~

Tony was reeling that Anna ditched dinner. He tried to hide it but knew he wasn't fooling anyone. His jaw was tense, his face tingled with perspiration, and his body was rigid. He loved her family, and of course, Elizabeth, but Anna was the reason he came.

"Tony, can I see you in the kitchen for a minute?"

Several pairs of inquisitive eyes were fixed on him as he followed Helena. She wasted no time before diving in.

"Do you like my daughter?"

"We are good friends."

"If that's it, fine, but if not, you better tell her how you feel. Because my daughter never misses a family gathering, but someone convinced her to spend more time with him tonight."

Gina walked in then, and Tony suspected she heard the tail end of that conversation. Could this night get any more awkward?

"Hey, Mom. Can I talk to Tony alone for a minute?"

"Sure, why don't you guys head over to John's den where no one will bother you while I stay here and finish dinner?"

Tony followed her back and realized he didn't have those same feelings from when they were together. No fluttering in his abdomen, no quickening of his heartbeat. Was it because of her sister-in-law? When they arrived in the dimly lit room, filled with all of John's police paraphernalia, he sensed the awkwardness immediately. It dawned on him that this was the first time they were alone since they dated. Before he could say anything to break the silence, Gina beat him to it.

"Tony, I don't want us to feel uncomfortable around each other."

His shoulders relaxed, and he sensed a similar reaction in her.

"I don't either, Gina. I'm happy for you and Christian—he has always been one of my good friends. I'd like for all of us to try to be friends. Do you think we can do that?"

"Of course, especially if you're going to be dating Anna."

"Oh, come on, not you too."

"We all know it, Tony. And she's not supposed to be with Garrett either. She has never missed a family dinner—and especially not for some guy she has gone on a few dates with."

He stood immobile, not wanting to give anything away by the emotions building inside him. He balled his fists and pressed his feet into the floor to ground him.

"You know I'm right."

"I don't, Gina. You just said I'm not exactly impartial here. Maybe they are perfect for each other."

"That's a lie, and you know it."

Just then, Helena gestured from down the hall that it was time for dinner. When Gina turned to leave, he took her arm ever so slightly. "Gina, thanks for putting me at ease. But I have to admit I feel weird going in there and having dinner with your parents."

"You're silly. And they are on team Tony and Anna, so don't sweat it."

He rolled his eyes and followed her down the hall, realizing he was breathing a little easier.

Chapter 10

Anna returned from Garrett's and contemplated who to text first. Everyone was mad at her—Mom and Dad, Gina and Christian, and she didn't blame them—especially Gina. She adored Gina's parents, Sal and Maria, and couldn't believe she canceled to be with Garrett. They had a good time together, watching a movie. He kept trying to get closer to her, but she just wasn't there yet. She enjoyed being around him but wasn't ready for more and tried not to dissect why.

Of all the people she should have called first, she dialed Tony. When he didn't pick up, she left a voicemail apologizing for the position she put him in and that she hoped he could forgive her. Before hanging up, she promised to see him at the game on Tuesday.

Her mother would have to wait another day, so she fired off a quick text apologizing and telling her she would stop by one day this week.

Next, she called Gina's house phone and was both relieved and disappointed when Christian picked up.

"Calling to grovel, sis?"

"Stop it. Where's Gina?"

"I'll go get her, but you better apologize. You know how much she missed you and how much she was looking forward to today, and you blew her off."

"I know! Just get her on the phone."

"Hey," was all Gina said.

"Gina, I'm so sorry. I don't know what else to say. I wanted to see your parents. I don't know what came over me, but I hope you can forgive me."

"Of course. But now I'm worried about you—I don't want Garrett changing you, Anna."

"I'm still the same person. That's not fair."

"The Anna I know would have never done what she did today."

She felt guilty enough without everyone piling it on, so she tried to change the subject.

"Dare I ask, how Tony was? I just called him, and he didn't answer."

"It's obvious he's upset. But in other news, we talked today and decided to be friends, and we let go of the awkwardness."

"That's great, Gina," she said, while inside, the fact made her a little jealous.

"Listen, I'm going to let you go, but I'm sorry. Let's get together soon."

"Are you going to Tony's game on Tuesday? If yes, Chris and I will see you there."

"Great, see you then." Why was she suddenly feeling like an outsider in her own family?

~

Tony let the phone ring. He didn't want to talk to Anna, but now he was eager to listen to the voicemail. His hurt melted away at the sound of her gentle voice apologizing and wishing him luck on Tuesday. As much as he wanted to stay mad, he never could. He thought of her leaving the message, tucking her hair behind her ear, as was her habit, especially when she was nervous. He realized he couldn't wait until Tuesday, which is why he hit her name on his phone before changing his mind.

"Hey, I'm glad you called."

"Did you enjoy your day?" He heard the gruffness in his tone but made no apologies. "Tony."

"What? You called to talk. Tell me about your day." He knew he was making her uncomfortable. He could hear her subtle sighs through the line.

"I shouldn't have ditched dinner, especially when I was the one who convinced you to come to my parents today. I'm really sorry. I made a rash decision, and I regret it."

"Did you at least have fun?" Why was he torturing himself like this?

"I did. I just got off the phone with Gina. I heard you guys cleared the air." She seemed annoyed when she said it, but he couldn't figure out why. There was no way she was jealous of her sister-in-law, who was happily married with two kids to Anna's brother.

"We did, and it's a huge load off my shoulders."

"Do you still have feelings for her?"

"Anna!"

"What?"

"Why are you acting like a jealous girlfriend?"

She didn't respond, but he needed to know the answer, and frustration built with every second. "Listen, Anna, I'll see you at the game Tuesday," then he hung up without giving her a chance to say goodbye.

~

Tony knew the minute she sat down in the bleachers

at the high school. He was aware of her presence, even before Christian yelled his name. There were only a few dozen people there as the game wouldn't start for another 20 minutes. But Tony knew Christian would arrive early to watch the warm-ups. So, when he looked their way, he barely noticed Gina and Chris. He honed in on Anna in a pair of jean shorts, a white tank top, showing off her tanned Mediterranean skin, and long dark hair in a tight ponytail, and his breath caught. She gave him a wave, flashed her signature smile, and all his anger evaporated. He prayed Brandon didn't see how she affected him while they stood together looking over the notes for today's game. Tony had written down all the things they had to beware of, and on the top of the list was the killer curveball of their opponent's starting pitcher. The kid already committed to Vanderbilt, one of the top-ranked teams in the country. Brandon, the team's ace, had to hit his spots and leave nothing hanging over the middle as the lineup he faced today led the conference in home runs the last three seasons. So Tony was shocked when he turned to him with a smirk on his face. "That's the girl, isn't it, coach? She's the one that has you all tied up in knots."

"Don't you think you should have your attention on the game?"

"That is all I'm thinking about. Don't worry about me. I just hope your head is in it."

Did his player just question him? But most importantly, was the answer yes? He made a point at that moment not to look toward the stands until the game was over. He had to stay focused on his team and make sure they delivered a win. If they were headed to States, they needed to claim every game.

~

Anna wondered if Tony could hear them cheering from where he paced on the field. Even though they were almost at the top row, the three of them were loud, but then again, so was the crowd. After all, the game was a nail-biter. It was the last inning, and they were down by one run and already had two outs. Tarpon had to score now, or they would lose. When number seven came up to bat, Anna was hopeful. She knew he was having a good day at the plate as he already racked up three hits and four RBIs. She looked around and saw everyone hunched forward in their seats, some biting their nails, others pressing her fingers to their temples. When the count went 0-2, her hope faltered. But when he took the third pitch deep to center field and the ball headed to the outfield, the crowd jumped from their seats. The ball bounced off the top of the fence. Everyone erupted in cheers as the runner on third headed home, followed by the runner on second base. The center fielder, who boasted a rocket for an arm, launched the ball from the warning track, hitting the catcher's glove on one hop. The runner slid under the tag. "Safe," said the umpire in a manner that commanded respect. The fans went nuts, and Anna, Christian, and Gina hugged each other while high-fiving simultaneously.

They stayed in the bleachers as they knew Tony would have to talk to the team before they could congratulate him. Anna's eyes never diverted from Tony's spot on the field and realized it too late. Gina leaned in and whispered, "Still claiming you have no feelings?"

"He's my friend. I'm happy for him."

"Enough to give him a congratulatory hug?"

"You know you guys are making this awkward for me."

"I'm sorry. I'll stop."

"Thank you. Look, they are starting to break from the huddle. Let's go." Her brother was already several steps ahead of her. His long stride and exuberance for the sport propelled him toward the field.

"Congrats, Coach," said Christian as he took one of his hands to shake while giving him a half hug with his other arm. Since Gina was standing next to Christian, she was next, and it took everything Anna had not to be jealous when they embraced as well. Then the couple took off, her brother muttering something about saying hi to the assistant coach.

"Congratulations," Anna said, pulling him in for a hug of her own. "You did it!"

"They did it. I'm so proud of them."

Just then, Anna saw number seven, and the pitcher headed over.

"Hey Coach, introduce us to your friend," said Brandon.

Did Tony just scowl at his two players who delivered the win?

"Anna, this is Brandon and Dean. Meet my friend Anna."

She saw Brandon's crescent eyebrows raise when Tony called her a friend. She tried not to read too much into it.

"Great game, guys. That was amazing."

"Thanks," they both said in unison. "We have an awesome coach," said Brandon.

"Yeah, yeah," said Tony, shooing them away. Don't

you have parents to go find?"

"See ya," said Dean.

"Nice meeting you, Anna," said Brandon.

"I'm proud of you, Tony. I know you work hard with these kids, and it shows."

"Thanks. It means so much to me that you came."

"Of course!"

As much as she wished the awkwardness wasn't there, she knew he still ached from her actions the other day. It was evident that she hurt him and vowed right then to make it right. She could see other parents standing awkwardly to the side, waiting to offer their congratulations, and she didn't want to monopolize him.

"Well, listen, Coach, I can see there are a lot of people eager to applaud you. Can we talk this week?"

"Sure, Anna. Thanks again."

"Anything for you, Tony."

Several hours later, Tony had finally showered, scarfed down two salami and provolone sandwiches, and was relaxing on the couch. Well, not exactly relaxing. He was furiously making notes for their next face-off two days from now. He wondered if Anna would be at that game too. He couldn't get her out of his head, no matter how hard he tried.

Anything for you, Tony.

Was he reading into that comment? It didn't seem like a statement she would make to just anyone. Just then, Elizabeth's name lit up his phone screen.

"Hi, Elizabeth."

"Hey, Tony, congratulations. Both Gina and Anna texted to tell me about your big win today. I'm so proud of you."

"Thanks, it was pretty awesome."

When she didn't say anything else, he knew she wasn't calling just to say congrats. And he wanted to pick her brain about Anna. "Spit it out."

"What?"

"Fine, if you won't start the talk about Anna and me, I will."

"Wait, I thought you said there was no you and Anna."

"I'm ready to admit it—but only to you, and you have to keep it quiet."

"Fine, but everyone knows. It's so obvious you two like each other. I don't know what that girl's problem is. Actually, I do."

"Garrett?"

"Yeah."

"Today, when she left, I told her thanks for coming, and she said she would do anything for me. Do you think that means something?"

"Duh, of course, it does!"

"Then why is she still dating him?"

"We've been over this before. Garrett is pursuing her. A girl likes that. And his looks don't hurt."

"Gee, thanks."

"I didn't mean ..."

He was getting all worked up now, and feeling insecure, an emotion he never experienced until Anna. His looks have never been a problem—girls always found him attractive and even asked him out. But he could never find someone who shared his same faith—until Gina. And now that Anna found the Lord as well, thanks to her sister-in-law, he was hoping maybe she was the one. That and a million other reasons is why he was drawn to her—her kindness, exuberance for living life, and that smile. She had so much beauty and was utterly unaware of it.

"I didn't think Anna was shallow. Do I seriously have to hit the gym for her to notice me?"

"Tony."

"I'm serious."

"I don't know. I think it's the whole package that drew her in—his looks—the fact that he's in the worship band. She just thinks he is perfect, even though the way he has treated her doesn't live up to the façade he has built up."

His heart rate was now sky high, and he paced around the room needing to move—to do something. "I've been told I'm not bad to look at. I love the Lord, and she knows that! What do I have to do to get her to notice me?"

"Whoa!"

"What?"

"I knew you liked her, but I had no idea it was this much. You have to tell her."

"I won't. I'm not competing with that guy. It's not worth it. She needs to figure this out for herself."

"Are you coming to dinner on Sunday? Helena says we have a standing invite."

"I can't, Elizabeth. I need to put some space between us. Now that I admitted my feelings, I realize it's too hard to be around her. It's like what happened with Gina all over again.

"Tony!"

"It's fine. Listen, thanks for calling, but I'm beat. I'll talk to you later."

TARA TAFFERA

"I'm coming to your game on Thursday."

"Awesome, see you there."

~

Elizabeth got off the phone and texted Grace and Gina. "I'm sorry to gossip, but I have to tell someone. I just talked to Tony. He has it bad for Anna, but I can tell he's starting to give up. What do we do?"

"Nothing," said Grace. "Anna has to figure this out for herself."

"But what if she doesn't?" answered Elizabeth.

"We support her, no matter what."

"Really?" questioned Gina, entering the conversation. "I'm starting to realize how perfect those two are for each other. You should have seen them at the game. They hardly talked, but their eyes said it all."

"Garrett doesn't seem like the one for her, but she has to figure it out on her own," said Grace.

"What if he hurts her?" asked Gina.

"God will protect her."

"I hate it when you're right."

Grace sent back a smiley face emoji and said good night.

"Well, I am always saying God has a plan. I need to listen to my own words," said Gina.

"Easier said than done," said Elizabeth.

~

The day after the game, Anna still couldn't stop thinking about Tony but felt her smile form when she saw Garrett calling her.

"Hey, Garrett."

"Hey, babe. What are you doing on Saturday?"

"No, plans right now. Maybe boarding in the morning."

94

"I have a competition this weekend, and I would love for you to come, and this one is close—over in Tampa."

She liked Garrett but watching a bunch of guys all greased up and flexing their biceps and triceps didn't sound all that exciting. She giggled inwardly. On second thought, maybe Elizabeth would want to go with her.

"Babe?"

"Sorry. I want someone to come with me since you'll be busy competing. Let me ask Liz and get back to you."

"Okay, but I really want you there. I went paddleboarding with you."

Did he seriously just say that? Is he comparing a few hours on the water to sitting in a stuffy gym all day? And it's not like she would even see him much—it's totally different.

"Let me call her later, and I will get back to you."

And that was that. He didn't ask about her week. Nothing. He hung up and said he would wait for her call.

~

Anna was surprised Liz agreed so quickly to join her today. She knew her friend didn't like Garrett, but apparently, the promise of more than a hundred guys flexing their pecks all day was too hard to turn down. Anna scanned the room, searching for Garrett, but it was hard to pick him out—they all kind of looked alike—similar builds, fake tans.

Garrett surprised her from behind and wrapped his arms around her possessively. She predicted Liz would be commenting on that later. Anna was not big into public displays, and her friend knew it. But just as quickly, he turned to embrace Elizabeth as well.

"Thanks for coming with Anna," he said while leaning in to give her a peck on the cheek. "If you see anyone you like, let me know. I can find out if they are single."

Anna noticed Liz didn't even try to hide her delight, which was evident from the raising of her thin, perfectly groomed eyebrows. She simply gave a nervous chuckle in return.

"I wish I could talk, but I have to go warm-up. I'll be taking the stage over here around ten for the first round of the day."

"Good luck."

"Thanks, babe. I'm so happy you're here."

As soon as he was out of earshot, she knew Elizabeth would start in. "Hey, babe, what's up? Love ya, babe."

"Stop!"

"I'm teasing. I just didn't know you all were at that stage."

"What stage?"

"I don't know. Pet names."

"Babe is not a pet name. You're unbelievable."

"Anna Andros, are you blushing? Wow, so you do like this guy?"

"I've been telling you that."

"Yeah, but I guess I didn't believe you. And I didn't like some of the ways he has treated you."

"Neither did I, but I'm giving him another chance."

"I hope he doesn't blow it. Let's go get a front-row seat. Garrett did tell me to tell him if I was interested …"

"Oh, brother," said Anna, as she laughed and thought the day and her relationship with Garrett was looking up.

A few hours later, Garrett came over to tell them he made it to the semifinals, but it would be at least an hour until that round began.

"Elizabeth, would you mind if I stole Anna away for a few minutes?"

"Of course. I have to make a few calls anyway. I'll head outside to get some air."

Anna gave Elizabeth a look. "Who am I kidding? I'll go sit in my air-conditioned car."

Anna laughed, and Garrett pulled her into a corner, surprising Anna. He hadn't hid his feelings for her and definitely was a toucher, but he hadn't kissed her yet. Was he going to do that here around a bunch of sweaty bodybuilders? An announcement broke up their playful banter and easy conversation.

"Sorry, Anna, that's my signal," then he bent down to her level and barely touched her lips with his. Before she could process what happened, she spotted Liz by the door with an apprehensive smile.

"Did he just give you your first kiss here?"

"What does it matter? I thought you were starting to like him."

"I was, but I don't know. I just wonder if he's being a little showy."

"What does that even mean? Let's go get our seats." Once again, Liz didn't see the multitude of eyes on her as she walked away.

~

A few hours later, the competition had ended, and Anna and Liz were waiting for Garrett to come back out after the finals, where he came in second. Anna had no idea what they based these things on, but she figured second place was good. It seemed all they did was get up on stage and flex their muscles, but there must be more to it than that. She would have to ask him later. She saw him walk away from his trainer and toward her with a scowl on her face.

"Hey, congratulations."

"For losing?"

"I'm sorry you didn't take first, but I am proud of you. We were just saying how much fun we had today watching you, even though we had no idea how any of this works."

"Clearly, because if you did, you would know that second is not an option."

She stared at him while telepathically sending a message to Liz to stay silent. She should have known better.

"Sorry you lost, Garrett, but don't take it out on Anna."

"Shut up and stay out of it."

It took a second for Anna to process what he just said. "What's wrong with you? What are you, five? Come on, Liz."

Anna knew he wouldn't be stopping them. When they got in the car, Liz finally opened her mouth. "Thanks, Anna."

"For what, calling him out? I'm so sorry he did that to you."

"I was just starting to like him. And I know you were falling for him even more after today."

"Yeah, until his rude side came out again."

"You okay?"

"I will be. But do I have to go to church tomorrow? And speaking of which, I can't believe a guy who leads the praise and worship every week just treated us like that. If I can't find a nice guy there, then what's the point?"

Liz just stared at her. "What?"

"You seriously have no idea?"

"Zero."

"You have to figure it on your own, Anna."

Chapter 11

Anna scanned the sanctuary and found Liz and Tony in their usual spot, then her eyes landed on Gina and Christian, and she immediately smiled. She headed straight to her brother and his wife and embraced them tightly.

"I see how it is," said Elizabeth.

"Oh, come on, I saw you yesterday."

"You didn't see me yesterday."

"Hey Tony," she said with a bright smile.

She sat between her two girlfriends, and Elizabeth leaned in and whispered, "I thought you weren't coming today."

"I wasn't. Then I realized how stupid that would be. I love coming here each week. I'm not letting him take that away from me."

The music started then, and Garrett looked right into her eyes, gave her a wink, and flashed her a look that could melt any girl's heart. Was he really acting normal? She glanced at Liz, who clearly saw what transpired by the "what the heck was that?" expression on her face.

When the pastor delivered his sermon, he seemed to be speaking right to her. She was sure others thought the same, but it was what she needed to hear today. It was all about keeping your eyes fixed on Jesus, praying, and asking for guidance, and making Him the center of your life. Had she been doing that in the past few months, or was she so focused on looking for a guy to fit into the boyfriend/husband timeline she set for herself that she forgot to turn to God? When the sermon was over, she felt a sense of calm until she saw Garrett walking toward her. She grabbed Liz's arm and noticed that Tony saw her do it.

"Hey Anna, hey Elizabeth, thanks again for coming yesterday."

When neither Anna nor her friend replied, Christian filled the silence by stepping forward and offering his hand.

"I'm Christian, Anna's brother, and this is my wife, Gina."

"Hello," was Gina's only greeting, and Anna noticed she was sizing him up as only a best friend and sister-in-law would. Anna couldn't believe Garrett was still standing there. If this was happening to her, she would have scurried away in embarrassment. Who was she kidding? He had nerves of steel and confidence to match, as she witnessed yesterday. She realized he might not even be fazed by the awkwardness blanketing everyone else like a plague.

"It's nice to meet Anna's family finally. I still haven't been able to wrangle an invite to your weekly dinners on Sunday."

"I wouldn't be too offended. Anna missed last week for you—something she has never done. I think my mom is still steaming. You should probably wait until she calms down more before Anna brings you over."

Anna noticed that's what tipped him over the edge to annoyance. She would thank her brother later. She glanced at Tony to see him standing like a statue and realized he never acknowledged Garrett. Or was it the other way around?

"Well, when I meet your mother, I will be sure to apologize for her daughter's absence and will take full responsibility. But I didn't force Anna to ditch dinner."

This guy was unbelievable. She had to get out of here.

"We better get going. See you, Garrett."

"Nice meeting you all. I hope to see you soon."

"Not if I can help it," she heard Tony mutter under his breath. She let everyone walk ahead and noticed Garrett headed toward the rest of the lunch crew, then saw him talking and flirting with a few girls from their Bible Study. She touched Tony lightly on the arm, urging him to stop. "Did I just hear you correctly?"

"What?"

"Don't play dumb."

"Anna, I have no idea what happened yesterday, but clearly you saw him, and I can tell he hurt you—yet there he is acting like nothing is wrong—and wanting to meet your parents. If you won't stand up for yourself, maybe you need someone to do it for you."

Before she could respond, he kept going. "We all know you're easy-going. But that doesn't mean you can let that guy walk all over you."

"Thank you."

His eyes blinked, and his head seemed to shake slightly as if he wasn't sure he heard correctly. He glanced down where she was still touching his arm but made no move to pull it away.

"You're not mad?"

"Why would I be mad when you are looking out for

me?"

He smiled. "Because I've done it before, and you went nuts."

"That was different. You thought he was cheating on me when he was out with his sister."

"True. Listen, I have to go, but are you okay? It looks like he may come back over here. Do you want me to wait with you?"

"No, I'm good; we're in church. I don't think it will get ugly here of all places," she joked.

"Okay, text if you need anything. Will I see you at the game Monday?"

"Yes, but aren't you coming to dinner today?"

"Nah, I am spending the day with my parents. And even if I wasn't, I'm going to let you deal with your mother all by yourself."

"Gee, thanks for being such a great friend."

He gave her a wave, and when she turned back around, Garrett had almost reached her. "Anna, are we okay?"

"You must be joking." The dumbfounded look on his face told her he wasn't. "You really aren't going to apologize to me? I'm surprised you didn't do it earlier when Elizabeth was here, as you owe her one too."

"For what?"

Suddenly, she wasn't just angry at him but herself for ever seeing any redeeming quality in this guy.

"Garrett, we had a lot of fun yesterday, but then you lost and treated both of us poorly."

"Come on, babe, that's how everyone acts when they lose."

"No one I know behaves like that."

"You must not know many competitive athletes

then?"

She wasn't going to get into this with him—especially not in a house of God. But she wanted to shout about Tony, her brother, all competitive baseball players, who would never act as juvenile as he did when he came in second place.

"I know a lot of them, and I was once one myself."

Her brother wasn't the only one with athletic genes. She played volleyball all through high school and was a top-ranked player. Even though she didn't have the height of a typical hitter, she had a powerful arm and a jump height that most of her taller teammates envied.

"And my brother and Tony were the stars of the high school baseball team. And now Tony is the coach, and they are on their way to States. But if they lose, he won't act like you did yesterday—nor will his players."

"So, this is about Tony. Why does every fight we have come back to him?"

"I'm ignoring that, as you know it's not true." He was getting under her skin, and her next words came out before she could stop them.

"And you know what else? I'm surprised you didn't apologize. But even more surprised given where we are right now, and that you call yourself a man of God."

"Fine, I liked you, Anna, but it's over. I can't live up to the impossibly high standard you set for me."

That doesn't say a lot about the women he has dated in the past. The old Anna would have told him that. The one who found God kept it to herself—while biting her lip. After all, she was still human. When she arrived back at her car, she let out a breath at the sight of Tony leaning against her Accord.

"I was about to come in after you. Is everything

okay?"

"I thought you had to meet your parents."

"I couldn't leave without making sure you were alright. Are you?" She nodded her head. It was obvious he didn't believe her, and Anna realized how well he knew her. He must have decided not to push, which she appreciated. He simply shot her that dazzling smile, waved goodbye, then drove off in his truck, leaving her looking after him.

~

With each step closer to his parents door, the tension left his body bit by bit. The scent of homemade pasta and meatballs filled the air, and he couldn't wait to indulge later after he helped his dad in the yard.

"There's my boy," said his mother Lydia, walking out of the kitchen wearing her red apron dotted with flour.

"Hey, Ma. I can smell the meatballs, but judging from the flour on your shirt, are we having homemade pasta too?"

"Gnocchi."

"Yum. I better go get Dad so we can get this work over with and eat." He knew better to think he would escape some questions from his mother, but it was worth a shot.

"Come, sit, and talk to your mother first. Your dad is still taking his sweet old time changing from church. And when he comes down, it will be all baseball talk." Here it comes.

"How was church?"

"It was good. The sermon was powerful, and everyone was there today—everyone from the Andros family, Elizabeth too—so it was nice to see them all."

"That's nice, dear," she said while patting his hand. "So, why are you spending time with us instead of going out for lunch with those nice people?" He knew she wanted him here, and if he didn't come, she would have complained about that, so he knew she was fishing.

"I can leave if you want. I can always go to Christian's mom's later and eat all her amazing Greek food." She slapped his hand away while wearing a huge smile, and he flashed her one of his own.

"So, are you dating anyone?"

"Wow, Mom, you don't waste any time."

"I told you your father is going to be down here any minute and whisk you off to work and talk about your team. I need to get you while I can." The only girl he wanted to date was Anna. He thought of how beautiful she looked this morning when she walked to his truck. He donned his sunglasses so she couldn't see that his eyes never wavered from her. Every time he saw her, his heart beat faster, and it was impossible to look away. Yes, she was beautiful with her dark hair and smoldering eyes, but it was more than that. She had a quality that drew people to her. He looked up to find his mother staring at him with a knowing glance.

"So, who is the lucky girl?"

Then his dad walked in, and Tony could breathe again. He wasn't ready to talk about his feelings for Anna.

"Leave the boy alone, Lydia." Tony got up and embraced his dad in a quick hug.

"Hey, old man, let's get these jobs done so I can enjoy Mom's meal."

"Give me a minute. I am an old man. Let me sit and

talk to you before we head out to the yard."

Tony let the comment go, even though his dad was anything but old. His parents hadn't even hit 60 yet. He enjoyed this time with them, though, so he settled in for the baseball talk while his mom got up to stir the sauce and prep the dough.

"Did your mom tell you we will be at the game tomorrow?"

She hadn't, and now he worried about keeping his feelings for Anna to himself. Those sunglasses would come in handy again.

"No, she was too busy grilling me about women." His dad rolled his eyes. "I'm glad you two can make it."

"Your last game was your toughest match-up, I think. You pulled that off. But this one is going to be challenging too. Don't let your guard down."

Tony was well aware and would heed his dad's advice. This opponent also made it pretty far last year, and Tony had been following their star pitcher, a kid with a powerful arm headed to a D-1 school.

"Believe me, I know. Christian and I were talking about it today after church. But we're ready."

"I'm proud of you, son. How is Christian?"

"He's great. He and Gina came to the last game, but she won't be there again tomorrow, you know, with the kids and all. But Anna will be there with her brother."

His mom stopped rolling the gnocchi dough and turned toward them. "How is Anna? It will be so nice to see both of them."

"They are good. We spend a lot of time together— Elizabeth too. She may be there, but I'm not sure."

His Dad stood up suddenly, perhaps sensing his

wife was about to ask if Tony had any interest in either of the girls.

"Well, that yard needs a lot of work. You ready, son?"

"Just don't kill me before the game tomorrow." Then he gave his mom a quick kiss on the cheek, breathed in the scent of the sauce again, and his mouth watered once more.

~

Tony walked toward his players, who were already out on the field getting ready for warmups. "What's with you, Coach?" asked Brandon. "You look like you can hardly walk."

"Three hours of yard work."

"You must be getting old."

"Watch it."

He couldn't believe how sore he was from yesterday. All that bending uses muscles you didn't know you had—and he was in shape. He wondered how his dad was faring. Just then, he saw his parents walking toward the stands and went over to greet them. He noticed his dad's step was as spry as ever.

"How are you not walking slower? I'm so sore from yesterday."

"I guess I'm in better shape than you."

Tony ignored that comment and told them to head over to their seats as he had to get back to the team. They wished him good luck and said they would pray for a successful game and everyone's safety.

A few hours later, they were in the last inning, and his team was up by two runs, and the opponent only had one out left and no one on base. If they could get the final out, they would have another victory in the bag. It had been a close game, and Tony was laser-focused and realized he hadn't looked up at the stands once. Now that he did, he saw Anna and Christian sitting with his parents. Anna didn't even notice him as she was engrossed in conversation with his mother. He moved his attention back to the game just in time as the batter connected with the ball, which shot to the outfield. But his left fielder glided over and caught it effortlessly as if he had done it a million times before. The fans erupted in victory, and Tony said a silent prayer of thanks to God before heading over to congratulate his players. Once his guys dispersed to get their congratulations from friends and family, Tony walked over to his parents and friends.

"Great job, son. You handled that one with ease."

"Thanks, Dad. I'm glad all of you were able to make it." He tried not to look Anna's way, as he knew his mom would be watching his every move, wondering if Anna could be the one to get her boy to settle down and give her grandchildren. He was determined not to provide her any ammunition.

"Why don't we all go out to eat to celebrate? Our treat," his mom offered.

He noticed Anna look tentatively at her brother. "I have to get back to the family, but thanks so much for the offer. Gina's been home long enough, and I need to give her a break. Eva's teething now, and it's been rough. But you all go and have fun."

Tony looked at Anna. "Sounds fun," she said. He was thrilled and apprehensive all at once. How was he going to hide his feelings under his mother's perceptive and watchful stare?

"Wait, I just realized, Christian was my ride."

"I'll drive then drop you after dinner. Mom, where are we going?"

"You decide, Coach, you're the star today." He shook his head at his mother.

"I could go for pizza. Want to meet at that brick oven place downtown?"

"Sounds good. See you there."

Tony and Anna walked toward the car and passed Brandon.

"See ya, Coach. Hey, Anna."

"Wow, how does he remember my name?"

Tony ignored her comment while vowing to make him run an extra mile tomorrow. They reached the car, and he realized he was sweaty just from warming up with the team and enduring the heat. He pulled out the extra shirt he always kept in the car for these occasions.

"Give me a second," he told Anna. "Believe me; no one wants me to stay in this smelly shirt. He saw her looking at her phone while he pulled off his coach's jersey and put on a fresh polo.

Once they arrived at the restaurant, Tony forgot all about the possibility of his mother's stares. They had so much fun together, and he realized yet again how right and easy it felt to be around Anna. However, when they finished their pizza, Tony noticed a twinkle in his mother's eye as she leaned into Anna.

"I'm so glad we got to know you, dear. Since high school, it's been a long while when Tony and Christian were on the baseball team, and I would see you at games. You have grown into a lovely woman."

Tony noticed the blush that immediately flooded her cheek. "Thank you, Mrs. Donelli. I enjoyed

LOVE UNFAILING

spending time with you and your husband as well."

"Well, we should be going. And, son, you need to go home and take a shower. You stink."

Tony was horrified until his dad swatted him on the back playfully. "Relax, I'm kidding. Enjoy some more time with this lovely lady. But your mother and I are going to head out."

"Thank you so much, Mr. Donelli," said Anna, getting up to give him and his mom a hug.

"I enjoyed it, Anna. I hope to see you again soon. Maybe in the playoffs?"

"I will be there," she said. "My brother and I plan to cheer them on all the way to States."

"Well, then I look forward to seeing a lot more of you."

Tony turned his attention back to Anna and noticed the look of contentment there. "Thanks so much for inviting me."

"Well, technically, it was my mom."

She looked over at him, and he noticed the confusion on her face until he broke into a sly grin.

"Jerk."

"Easy target."

He loved seeing her so relaxed, and he wished he could stay there forever. But his dad was right. He did stink.

"As much as I would love to hang out longer, I fear my dad is right. I think I need to go home and hit the shower."

"Of course. I'm sorry, I didn't mean to keep you."

He put his hand on hers. "You didn't. I'm glad my mom thought of this. It was fun."

~

111

Anna stood at the window watching Tony drive away, and the image of him switching out his shirts at the car flashed through her mind. While she was looking at her phone when he changed, she stole a glance at his toned abs. And his arms. Okay, maybe it was more than one glance, and now she was mortified that maybe he noticed. She had so much fun, though, and was already looking forward to seeing him Thursday at the next game. He was so easy to be around—but all friends are like that, she reasoned.

Chapter 12

Throughout the next week, Anna and Tony texted often, and since they had dinner with his parents, thoughts of him occupied an ample space in her mind. She was both nervous and excited for today's match-up, so she couldn't imagine how Tony felt. With every win, they made it closer to a chance at the State title. The community rallied behind them, and she knew she would have to arrive early to snag a good spot. The stands became more packed with each game.

She looked at her watch yet again, willing it to be time to leave and head to the high school. Of course, as soon as she said that, her email pinged. Edits just came back from Dan, her publisher, for today's deadline. She submitted that two days ago, and of course, he waited until the last minute to get it back to her. Fortunately for her, he didn't make many changes, so she fixed the few corrections, sent it off, and looked at her watch.

"Gina, wait up," said a voice from behind her. "Can I grab a ride from you? My car is acting up, and my girlfriend had to drop me at work today."

She looked at her colleague Nico with confusion. "Normally, I would, but I'm headed to a baseball game."

"I know, that's why I'm asking. I heard you talking to one of the other reporters about it this morning. Dan

113

just put me on the story."

His statement confirmed her theory about the excitement surrounding the team's quest for States. Still, all of this was keeping her from getting a good spot. She sent a quick text to her brother, telling him to save two seats.

"Sure, let's go." As they walked to her car, she turned to Nico, "Since when does Dan have you covering sports?"

"Since the sports reporter is overloaded, and Dan didn't realize until today all the hype around this game. So, what's your interest in it?"

"The coach, Tony, is a friend of mine. My brother will be there too. He used to play on the team with Tony several years back—which is the last time the school made it this far."

"Since I got this assignment an hour ago, I've been doing a little research, and this coach is impressive."

Pride welled up for Tony, but she attempted to conceal her emotions from her coworker.

Anna pulled into the high school parking lot, and her assumptions were correct—the lot was almost full. She was glad Christian texted her, confirming he saved them seats. She turned to Nico, "Wait, did you forget your camera? Dan's going to have your hide."

"No, apparently one of the dads is a professional photographer, and he and Dan are friends. He's going to send some shots to the paper later. We both know those will be way better than mine." She laughed, just as they found Christian, and she introduced the two men.

Tony wasn't out on the field yet, but she looked around and saw his parent's several rows away. She sent them a wave and a big smile, one they both returned in spades.

~

Tony walked out on the field, and while he was focused on his team, he wanted to find Anna. It gave him comfort to know where she was sitting in case he tried to seek out her beautiful face from time to time. His gaze found Christian, then Anna, but who was the guy she was talking to? Whoever, it was, his eyes were fixed on Anna's, and Tony's heart rate soared immediately—and not in a good way. She looked his way, flashed him that high-wattage smile, and waved, and Tony couldn't help but return the gesture. But then he turned back to his team, trying to get his attention back to them and not the guy staring at his girl.

~

Though this match-up was supposed to be a hard contest, his team headed into the bottom of the seventh up by two, and all they needed was the final three outs. That would make them undefeated for the season going into regionals next week. His players did their job, and the crowd erupted in cheers. His gaze found Anna, but her back was turned, and he caught her in a hug with the mystery man. Tony moved his gaze to Christian instead, who gave him an energetic fist bump in the air, making him smile, despite what he witnessed.

About ten minutes later, he saw Anna and her friend, or whatever he was, walking toward them. He wasn't feeling very friendly and wished he could turn the other way.

"Hey, Coach, congratulations," she said, pulling him into a hug he didn't return. Perhaps sensing the tension, she lengthened the space between them. "I wanted to introduce you to someone. This is Nico; he's covering the game for the paper and wants to talk to you for his article." She didn't let him answer before telling Nico she would wait for him at the car. She walked away without giving Tony a backward glance.

Tony silently berated himself as she walked away, her footsteps heavy. Anna and Garrett broke up due to his jealous tendencies, and now Tony was acting the same way—and they weren't even dating. He scolded himself silently, all while trying to answer Nico's questions about the game.

"Hey, I don't deserve the credit here. Can I grab my star pitcher, and you can talk to him?"

"That would be awesome. Thanks, Coach."

Tony waved to grab Brandon's attention, then asked Nico if he needed anything else from him. When he shook his head no, Tony took off to the parking lot, hoping to find Anna. She sat on the curb near her car, scrolling through her phone. Was she crying? Had he done that to her? Did she have feelings for him? Before he could ask any of those questions, she looked up at him, and all he saw was sadness, and that tore his heart in two.

"I'm sorry. I was a jerk."

"I know that. But why?" He sensed she already knew but was going to make him say it.

"I like you, and not just as a friend."

When she didn't say anything, he went on. "Every time I text or talk to you, I get butterflies. I thought maybe, finally, we could get our chance. I was going to talk to you about my feelings, and then you showed up with Nico."

"I didn't show up with Nico. I gave our sports

reporter a ride because his girlfriend wasn't available to drive him, and his car is acting up."

He opened his mouth to apologize again, but she held up her hand to stop him.

"I have feelings for you too, Tony. But then today, you go all caveman on me. That's why Garrett and I broke up."

"I know. I'm so sorry. I saw you, and I got jealous. Please forgive me." He spotted Nico walking toward them and wished for a few more minutes alone with her to explain.

"I need some time. Congratulations again, you deserve it." He opened the door for her, nodded goodbye to Nico, then watched her drive away without giving him another glance.

~

Anna threw herself on the couch and immediately composed a text to her friends. "Emergency girls night needed. Please say you all can come over tomorrow." The yeses came in immediately, but none of them, especially Elizabeth, wanted to wait, and they all tried to get an idea of what was going on. "I'll tell you everything when I see you." She just hoped they could help her figure out what to do next.

~

Elizabeth arrived first, followed shortly by Gina and Grace. Once they exchanged greetings, settled on her couch with an array of snack staples before them—cookies and chips, of course, Gina was the first one to dive in, surprising Anna. "We all know we love getting together, but something is on your mind, Anna. Spill it."

"I like Tony as more than a friend."

"That's your big news?" exclaimed Elizabeth. "Yeesh, I'm missing a new episode of 'This is Us' for this." Anna stuck her tongue out at her.

"I'm serious."

"We are, too," said Elizabeth. "We all know you like him. What made you finally realize it?"

She filled them in on the events of the past week, going to the games, texting more than usual, getting closer to him, and acknowledging their relationship extended beyond friendship. Gina was the next to speak.

"I'm sorry he acted like that, Anna. But you can't compare him to Garrett. Tony would never hurt you the way Garrett did."

"I know. Maybe I overreacted, but I was just so excited to see him. It's the first time we saw each other since things shifted between us, and this isn't how I wanted things to go."

"Do things ever play out the way we want?"

"Good point, Grace," said Anna. "So, what now?"

"You told him you needed time," said Liz. "So, take it. This is all-new, and things just ended with Garrett. I know things will work out with you two, but it's okay to go slow."

"Thanks, girls. You're the best. But tell me about you all. Gina, how are Eva and AJ?"

While Gina filled them in on how things were getting a little less insane at the Andros household, Anna relaxed and enjoyed this time with her girls. Gina looked less harried than usual, and joy overtook her as her sister-in-law filled her in on the latest antics with her niece and nephew.

"Are you getting more sleep now?" asked Grace.

"Anna doesn't have to kidnap you again, does she?"

"No, things are better. By the way, sorry I was such a jerk about that. Thanks for being there and knowing what I needed."

"Always, sis."

"Just so we are all on the same page," said Elizabeth. "Since we all hope Tony and Anna find their way together, Gina, you are good with this?"

"I'm more than good. Both Tony and Anna are amazing people, and I do hope God helps them find their way to each other."

"Wow, this girls' gathering just got a little sappy," joked Grace. "What else is going on? Anna, did your mother ever forgive you for ditching Sunday dinner?" Anna hurled a pillow at Grace as her answer.

"Hey, I would rather be sappy than talk about my mom being mad at me. I think as long as I don't do it again, she has forgiven me. And although she wants me to find a boyfriend, I know she's glad Garrett, and I are over."

"Wait until she finds out about Tony," said Gina, with a devious look in her eye.

"You wouldn't!"

"Anna, everyone knows you guys belong together. Even your mother," said Grace.

"Well, that doesn't mean I need to fill her in. If I do, that's all I will hear about." They all nodded their heads in agreement.

"I have a great idea," Gina exclaimed.

"About my mother?"

"No, sorry, you're on your own there," she said teasingly. "I've been in your mother's bad graces and not looking to take a trip back there. Anyway, sorry, I just had an idea about Tony and Anna and the next game. Why don't we all go? We are all friends with him, and that may help lessen the tension when Anna sees him again."

"I love that," said Anna, and the rest of the girls agreed. They would all meet on Friday for the first game in the regional match-up.

~

Tony stared at his phone as he had done for the last three days since he saw Anna. He said he would give her space, so he had to wait for her to reach out. But knowing that didn't make the ache in his heart any less painful. He loved that she had been showing up and cheering them on in the stands. He doubted she would be at regionals now after the way he treated her. That and her silence.

Trust in Me.

He heard the words clearly and realized his stupidity for not taking this to God days ago (or months ago) ever since his emotions for Anna intensified. He bowed his head immediately. "Dear Lord, please allow Anna to know how sorry I am. Let her heart heal so we can become friends again, and I can repair our relationship. Help us find our way together. Amen."

The sense of peace filled him immediately. Still, he hoped God's timeline matched up with his own because he didn't know how he could go much longer without talking to her.

~

Tony paced back and forth and reviewed his notes for the thousandth time. This opponent wasn't better than any they had faced previously, but the pressure was mounting. The stands were packed, and it was 15 minutes until the first pitch. He looked up and saw all his friends waving furiously at him. Anna wore a Tarpon High t-shirt, and he wondered if she dug that out from their high school days. Before he could catch her eye, Dean was standing next to him. Tony braced himself for the ribbing that would ensue, as Dean and Brandon loved teasing him about Anna. But his player was silent as he scanned the stands in search of someone. Tony patted him on the shoulder but didn't say a word. He knew he was looking for his parents, but Tony doubted they would be here if past games were any indication. The two talked briefly about some struggles at home, how his parents worked all the time, but Tony tried not to push. He was hoping Dean would open up to him more when he was ready. Tony looked over at the umpire, signaling the team take the field.

"You got this, kid. I believe in you."

"Thanks, Coach."

~

They went into the bottom of the seventh with the opponents up by one. These teams were so evenly matched that it had been close right from the first pitch. When one team scored, the other stepped up and did the same. The first hitter doubled, and Dean was up next. As he walked to the plate, Tony noticed his eyes once again scanned the stands. Tony tried not to judge Dean's parents for not being here for their son. The pitcher struck him out on three pitches—the first time that happened all season. Dean dejectedly headed back to the bench as the next hitter stepped into the batter's box. After swinging and missing on the first two pitches, he blooped a single to left field on the next one, moving the runner on second over to third. Now

Brandon was up, and Tony breathed a sigh of relief. He was his strongest under pressure. After the count went 0-2 on the first two pitches, Tony's nerves ramped up. But when Brandon connected on the next pitch, the line drive bounced off the wall in right-center, and both base runners scored. The crowd went nuts—only two more games now until States. Tony sent up a silent prayer thanking God for blessing the team once again.

It took almost 15 minutes for Tony to make it over to his friends, all standing ready with a hug or high-five. Though Anna had shot him a signature smile, she couldn't get too close as her brother was eager to talk about all the plays with Tony. Gina touched Christian lightly on the arm. "Okay there, slugger, let's let Tony talk to some other people too. You can rehash all the plays with him later."

Christian looked at everyone. "Sorry, you can tell I love this game."

"No one would have guessed," joked Elizabeth.

"Hey, there are your parents," said Christian. "I want to go say hi to your dad, then I will send them over here."

"Thanks, man."

"We'll go with you," said Grace. "I never met them and would love to." That left Anna and Tony alone, and he knew they looked like a bunch of shy high school kids.

"Great game. I'm proud of you."

"Thanks. I'm glad you came."

"Me too. I missed you."

"Really?"

There was so much more he wanted to say to her, but he saw Dean standing off to the side, and the guy looked downright dejected. "Listen, Anna, I want to talk to you so badly ..."

"I know," and she glanced over at his player and knew he needed someone to talk to. "Go."

"Thanks, Anna. Will you wait?"

"We'll see. Don't worry about me, Tony. He needs you."

He walked away, and Anna's heart swelled at what an amazing man he was. She looked around and no longer saw any of her friends, so she pulled out her phone and shot off a quick group text. While she waited for them to respond, she couldn't help stealing another look at Tony. He had his head bowed with Dean, and Anna could tell Tony was saying a prayer, and her heart burst again. Then the tears came as she realized the mistakes she made over the past few months. She headed toward her car before anyone could find her.

~

Anna sat on the couch with her phone and tried her best to dodge all the questions about why she disappeared today. She was ashamed of herself for her actions of the past few months. She was fawning over a guy just because he sang in church while ignoring the Godly man right in front of her. A text interrupted her thoughts, another from Tony. She couldn't bear to talk to him right now as she had no idea what to say.

"Answer the door, Anna."

"What?" Then she heard a knock and absentmindedly walked over and opened it. She wished she hadn't. His eyes darted to hers that were bloodshot, and she was sure tears stained her cheeks. He walked into her apartment, pulled her into his arms, and she started to cry once again.

He held her for a while before easing back slightly so he could look into her eyes. "Please tell me what's wrong. Did I upset you?"

She gestured for him to sit on the couch, and she took the spot on the other end, afraid to get too close to him. She started to talk but stared off in the distance, as she couldn't bear to look at him.

"Let me get this out, but please don't interrupt as I just need to say this, and it's hard for me." She saw him nod, and she continued. "I'm so utterly embarrassed. Here I was drooling over a guy I didn't even know because he sang in church, and I wanted a good guy. I'm a reporter. I know appearances can be deceiving, but I fell for him, and we all know how that turned out. And here I had you in front of me all along. You're humble, but you share your faith freely. You're a good guy!"

"Don't forget I'm not bad to look at either."

She felt the blush creep up her cheeks. "Hey, I told you to let me get through this."

"Sorry," he said with a grin, and somehow now she was able to face him.

"What I was going to say was, you have all these great qualities, and deep down, I think I knew how you felt about me, and I ignored you. And yes, you are not bad to look at."

Now maybe he was blushing.

"I'm sorry, I was so shallow. Can you forgive me?"

He reached his hand over and lay it on hers. "There's nothing to forgive."

"I have an important question, though." She looked at him expectantly, nervous for what he was about to ask. "I'm starving. Do you have any food?"

She laughed, and just like that, the tension evaporated, and her friend was back. And maybe now they could take that step toward something more.

"Do I have food? What kind of Greek would I be if I didn't? Besides, my mother always keeps me stocked." She started pulling containers out of the fridge, thinking another girls' night was in order. She had a lot to tell and was giddy about what the future may hold.

Chapter 13

Ever since the night Tony showed up at Anna's
doorstep, the two communicated incessantly. Tony still
hadn't asked her out on a proper date, but they hung out
at each other's houses on a few occasions, texted
several times a day, and spoke on the phone. Their
friendship was intensifying, and they both knew they
were on the road to a romantic relationship. But after
everything that happened, Tony was taking it slow.
Anna came to the latest game, and his heart melted
every time he saw her cheering in the stands. All that
was left now was the State championship. Even though
it was taking place a few hours away, his friends took
the day off and would be there to support him and the
team. Once the baseball season was over, he planned on
giving Anna his full attention. Until then, they were
getting to know each other more while engaging in
some harmless flirting in the process.

Tarpon High was earning a slew of press. Anna's
colleague had written such a good story that he was
now a permanent reporter on the road to the
championship. Tony got to know him better and really
liked him. Anna still talked to Nico at the games, but
Tony saw her constantly looking over her shoulder to
ensure she didn't make him jealous. Every time she did,
it was like a knife slicing through him. He prayed each

night that he would never hurt her again. The thought of Anna ever comparing him to Garrett in that way made him ill.

They still had to face Garrett each Sunday, which made things awkward. They always sat next to each other now, and while that happened before, Tony was extra paranoid. He didn't want to make things harder for Anna, as he knew Garrett still had a thing for her. Garrett didn't seem like the type of guy to let things go quickly. So Tony wasn't sure what he was thinking this past Sunday when he lightly took Anna's hand and guided her out of the sanctuary. They were standing by her car talking when Tony leaned in, gave her a kiss on the cheek, and told her he looked forward to seeing her at Helena's for dinner. As soon as he turned to find his own car, he came face to face with Garrett, who looked him square in the eyes with a malicious stare then walked away. A chill ran through him, almost as if he just encountered the Devil himself.

He walked away but not before looking back to make sure Garrett wasn't bothering Anna. When he saw him pull away, he felt comfortable enough to head toward his truck, knowing Anna was safe—for now.

~

Anna sat at the kitchen table, meticulously wrapping grape leaves. Her mother asked her to come by early to help, so they could spend time together. She may as well rip off the band-aid and fill her in on the events in her life. Or some of it anyway. She just felt so ashamed of it all—for falling for the wrong guy.

When she was about to open up, her dad walked in. "There are my girls. Do you need some help?"

"Hmph, he never asks me if I need help," teased

Helena.

"That's because you always shoo me away," he shot back. "And it looks like you are about to do it again."

"What a smart man you are, John Andros. As a matter of fact, I was about to have a little girl talk with our daughter. Is that okay?"

"Of course. I don't want to think about my precious girl dating anyone anyway. Unless it's Tony, of course."

"Well, in that case, pull up a chair, John."

"Mom!"

"Come on, Anna, you know how this family is. We've heard you have been getting closer to Tony, and we are thrilled. I can't think of a better man for you."

"It's not that easy, Dad."

"Love never is, darling."

"Love? We aren't even dating, really."

"Why not?" they both asked at once.

Anna decided to pour it all out. "Because I'm ashamed. There he was right in front of me, and I was all about appearances, and instead ran to someone I hardly knew who turned out to be a jerk. What does that say about me?"

"It says you are human and make mistakes," her mother answered.

~

Tony and Elizabeth rode to the Andros' together. No one answered when they knocked, so they let themselves in, something Helena and John had given them permission to do a while ago. But as they stood outside the door in silence and heard that conversation, Tony froze. Elizabeth gestured for him to step back. They made a big point of loudly opening the door, announcing their arrival.

"I'll get it," said Anna, jumping out of her chair.

Anna greeted them both, and Elizabeth announced she was going to see Helena and John.

"That was subtle," said Anna.

"We heard some of your conversation. She wanted to give me a minute to talk to you," then Tony stepped forward, closing the gap between them. He saw the blush even before it appeared—he was that in tune with her now and took a few more steps. Barely a few inches kept them apart. He put his hand on her cheek and tucked her hair behind her ear, and heard her breath catch.

"How much did you hear?"

"Enough to ask you a question. Anna, will you be my girlfriend?"

The smile that instantly took over her face told him she was in. "I will take that as a yes. See, now we are dating." Then he stepped back, and she sensed the gap immediately.

~

Tony knew they couldn't keep their eyes off each other all night, and everyone saw it, but he didn't care. The looks and a few conversations were all he had with her, though, as John and Christian were obsessed with the upcoming State Championship. That topic dominated most of the conversation.

After dinner and dessert, Christian and John headed to the sunroom to watch the Rays play. He knew they expected Tony to follow.

"Are you coming?" said John.

"Actually, Sir, I think I have had enough baseball for today. Would you mind if I took Anna away for an hour or so?"

"Of course not, son. I'm sorry we dominated the conversation with all the baseball talk. This should have been a break from all the pressure for you today."

"Yeah, sorry Tony, you know how we get," added Christian.

"No worries. I had a wonderful time. Mrs. Andros, thanks for a delicious meal, as always. Elizabeth, do you want me to come back and pick you up?

"Of course not. I'll get a ride. You two have fun."

Tony placed a soft hand on Anna's waist and guided her to the door. Once they were in his truck, he turned toward her. "Was that okay? I know this is going to be a crazy week, and I want to spend a little time with you before it gets too late."

"I wanted some time alone with you too." And although it was only a short ride to her house, she nestled closer to him. She rested her head on his shoulder, and Tony sent up a silent prayer thanking God for this simple moment.

~

On the morning of the State Championship, Anna felt like a kid again, so full of excitement. Elizabeth and Anna were in Alex and Gina's minivan on their way to Lakeland for the game. John was there too, and Helena was back at the house watching Eva and AJ. They were all decked out in the school colors and both excited and nervous for the day ahead. John and Christian talked about the article in the local paper yesterday that all but guaranteed the Bradenton team their victory.   Her brother turned to her, bringing her into the conversation and out of her daydreams about Tony.

"Sis, did the article bother him?"

"It didn't faze him. His players read it, though, and now they are all in their heads about it. That has him worried."

"They can't let it get to him," said John. "I do have to say, though, that his outfielder, the guy who is one of their best hitters, has been off his game lately. We really need him to be on today."

"That's Dean. He has troubles at home. The poor kid—his parents haven't come once. Before each game, you will see him look up in the stands hoping this is the one where they show up."

Anna noticed the deep scowl on John's face. "Well, I just became a member of Dean's fan club, and I'm making it my mission to cheer crazy loud for him today. Are you guys in?" They all yelled out a collective yes.

When they arrived at the large high school where the championship was held, Anna was blown away by the growing crowd. The magnitude of the game suddenly hit her, and she hoped Tony and the team could stay focused and not let all this get to them. They made their way down to the parking lot and saw the Tarpon team off to the side doing some stretches while Tony paced back and forth, seemingly lost in thought. She saw him stop, and he found her eyes and waved. She gave him a huge smile, which he returned in full. Then she noticed him look down at his phone, then heard a ping. "Hey, beautiful. Seeing you just calmed my nerves."

"You got this," she typed back. "Can't wait to see you after. Tell the team everyone here is rooting for them. Oh, and John made it is his mission to be Dean's official cheering section."

"That's awesome. The kid needs it. I can see him looking in the stands again for his parents. It breaks my heart. Listen, I gotta go, but thanks for coming. Can't wait to see you after."

She typed back, "Good luck," then saw Elizabeth smiling at her. "You got it bad."

"I know," then her friend leaned in and gave her a hug. She spotted Tony's parents and waved them over to sit with them. They all greeted each other and settled in for the game. Tony's dad Mario joined Christian and John to talk baseball while Lydia sat near the girls. "My son looks all calm out there, but inside I know the pressure is getting to him. He just cares so deeply, you know."

They all murmured their agreement, and Anna guessed his mother wasn't just talking about the team. Not subtle, but it made her happy just the same.

They arrived early enough to grab great seats. They were in the middle of the bleachers and right near the railing. She looked down and saw some middle school-age-looking kids making posters, and it gave her an idea. She yelled down to them, "Hey, do you have any spare posters? I'll pay you for it."

"We have an extra," they yelled back. "Come on down."

"Can I borrow your markers?"

"Sure. Who are you making a sign for?"

She looked over at John, and they both yelled at the same time. "Number 9!"

"He's awesome. Look, we made one for Dean too."

"Love it! We plan on cheering for him extra loud today."

"Cool. Us too."

132

Anna decorated her sign then got settled back in her seat in time for the national anthem to start.

~

It was the bottom of the third inning, and neither team had scored any runs, which she guessed meant they were evenly matched. The Tarpon team already had two outs by the time Dean came up to bat. He racked up two strikes quickly when she heard John yelling loudly. "Come on, number 9. You got this." The middle school kids were several rows over, but they heard John and started screaming and holding up their sign. It seemed the whole stadium of Tarpon fans joined in, and the noise was almost deafening. Anna looked down at him at-bat and witnessed the change in his demeanor right before connecting with the ball. It sailed deep into center field, and he took off. The crowd went nuts, and he made it safely to second base. Now it was Brandon's turn at the plate. He singled while Dean slid into third under the third baseman's tag.

The fans were on their feet now as the next batter came up. Anna turned to her brother. "How is this guy?" Christian gave her an iffy shoulder shrug back, and the nerves kicked in. But the kid singled on the first pitch while Dean came home, and Brandon moved to second. When Dean slid into home plate, they were all cheering so loudly, yet still, he searched the stands. Then his eyes stopped and connected with someone. Anna and John turned and saw two adults waving back wildly, yelling, "That's our boy!" Dean's smile was unlike one she had ever seen, and she wiped away her happy tear. Elizabeth nudged her from the side. "You're such a sap," as she rubbed a tear from her own lid.

The third inning gave Tarpon the momentum they

needed, and it was difficult for Bradenton to come back. The final score was 5 to 2, and the Tarpon crowd erupted when the last batter for Bradenton made the final out. People hugged and cheered, and Anna longed to congratulate Tony. But from the looks of the people storming the field, she would have to wait. They lingered in the stands when she saw who she assumed were Dean's parents walk toward their seats.

"Thanks for cheering on our son." Anna held out her hand and introduced herself as the coach's girlfriend. She liked the sound of that, by the way, then everyone else in her group said hello and congratulated them on what a great game their son played.

They grinned widely. "We were so glad to make it today. We both have crazy jobs and can't get much time off. But we told our bosses we were taking a vacation day as our kid was headed to States, and we needed to be there for him."

"I am sure he was thrilled you could make it," said John when they heard someone yell from the field. "Mom! Dad!"

"It was nice meeting you," then they both took off down the steps and enveloped Dean in their arms, and heaped on the praise.

Everyone in their group watched the exchange, then she looked up and caught Tony witnessing it too, and she knew that for him, that was the highlight of the game—even more than the win.

"Come on, people, let's go congratulate the coach," said Mario. They all took off down the steps, ran over to Tony, and took turns offering their hugs, high-fives, and congratulations.

"I know Tony has to take the bus home with the

team, but why doesn't everyone come over to my house later for a celebration dinner?" asked Lydia. "Christian, your players are invited, and John and Helena, of course." Everyone happily accepted the invitation, and then a group of parents started yelling for Tony to get in a team photo. He told everyone he looked forward to seeing them later then jogged toward the team. About ten minutes later, Anna heard her phone go off. "Can't wait to see you later. How awesome was it that Dean's parents came?"

"So amazing," she texted back. "I sensed that was the highlight for you."

"You know me so well. After my mom's, can you come over, so we can have some time together?"

"Yes!"

Chapter 14

Anna paced back and forth in her living room, waiting for Tony to arrive so they could spend the afternoon and evening together. The nerves and the butterflies were at war in her stomach. A week passed since States, and they talked or texted every day. But this was their official first date since they stood in her mom's foyer, and he asked her to be his girlfriend. At the sound of his car, Anna hurried outside and immediately flung her arms around him. He melted into her, then pulled back slightly without letting go.

"What was that for?"

"I missed you."

"Me too. I was nervous today, and I don't know why. I am always at ease around you. Thanks for reminding me of that."

"You're welcome."

"Ready to go?" he asked, eyeing the beach bag on her shoulder.

"Yes, let me just grab my paddleboard," she said when he stopped her.

"I got it, Anna," he said, picking it up and sliding it with ease into the back of his truck.

She spotted the one that was already there. "Did you borrow this?"

"I bought it. That way, when you invite me along,

I'm always ready."

Anna stood there looking at him and could sense his nervousness. "I'm sorry, there's no pressure for you to take me with you. I wanted my own, that's all."

"I think it's fabulous. Let's get on the road so we can enjoy this beautiful day."

Tony responded by guiding her to the passenger side with his arm around her waist. He gently closed her door, and she felt like a high school kid crushing on the cute boy in homeroom. They made the short drive to Treasure Island to paddleboard, relax on the beach and grab dinner. It was the perfect Florida day—80 degrees, but absent the crazy humidity that makes people hide in air-conditioned homes. They talked easily, and he held her hand for most of the drive. Not surprisingly, the city was packed, but they were lucky enough to find a prime spot near the beach to unload their gear.

"What do you say? Ready to try out that new board of yours?"

"You're on."

"Try to keep up," she yelled while heading off toward the water.

About an hour later, they were floating on their boards, soaking in the Florida sun. She wasn't compelled to fill the silence, and she again thought how comfortable she was around this man. Her eyes were closed as she sunbathed when she felt his finger softly take hold of one of hers. To Anna, the date couldn't get any better, even though they had hours ahead of them.

"Do you realize this is one of the few times we have been all alone?" she said.

"Why do you think I planned this day for us? It's

rarely just you and me."

"I like it."

"Me too."

She opened her eyes and found him staring at her.

"Hey, how long have you been watching me?"

"You're cute when you blush, you know."

"So are you," then she leaned over and kissed him lightly on the lips and watched the stunned look on his face and the redness appear on his cheeks.

"See, cute." Then she closed her eyes again and enjoyed the fact that Tony continued to hold her hand.

~

Just when Tony thought he had Anna figured out, she surprised him. Even though it was their first official date, he knew today was an opportunity for them to get closer. He was going to wait for the right moment to present itself, but maybe Anna had the same thoughts. Though it only lasted a second, and it was so slight, he could still feel the brush of her lips on his and couldn't wait for that to happen again.

"Ready to head back?" he asked her.

"Not really, but we probably should. I need more water."

"Me too. Race you?"

"See you at the beach."

They both arrived at the same time, breathless from trying to keep up with each other. He grabbed a cold bottle out of the cooler, handed it to Anna, then took one for himself.

"Hungry?"

"I am, but I want to find a restroom first."

"Go ahead, I brought some food for us, so I'll get it set up while you're gone."

He couldn't help but stare as she walked away. It wasn't until she was out of sight that he started unpacking his items, grapes, watermelon, crackers, and pepperoni, when he heard her behind him.

"Wow, this looks amazing."

She sat next to him on the blanket, and he handed her a plate, then made one for himself. They talked about their plans for the rest of the day: soaking up the sun for a while, taking a walk on the beach, then having dinner before driving home.

"I know we still have the afternoon ahead of us, but as far as first dates go, this is a pretty good one," she said.

"Pretty good, huh? I'll have to step up my game."

She winked, then lie back on the blanket beside him. He said a prayer of thanks that this beautiful, bold woman was finally seeing him as more than a friend.

~

A few hours later, they sat at an outside table just a few blocks down from their beach spot. They walked hand in hand, looking at restaurants along the way when they both agreed on the Italian café. Tony made his menu choice quickly, so he stared while Anna perused the selections. She looked up from her menu.

"What?"

"Just admiring the radiant woman I'm here with. Don't mind me."

She closed the menu and smiled. The waitress took their order and the next 15 minutes passed with ease. Anna asked him about Dean, and Tony told her they had been talking before or after class and that a high-profile college scout is recruiting him.

"That's amazing. Please tell him how happy I am."

"I don't know if I will."

She looked at him with surprise. "Why not?"

"Dean and Brandon like to tease me about you."

"Really, since when?"

"The beginning of the season. They knew right away how much I liked you."

"I'm sorry it took me so long to tell you."

He reached his hand across the table and stroked her palm with his thumb.

"I didn't say that to hurt you. I just mean I've liked you for a while, so that makes what's finally happening between us so special."

"What exactly is happening?"

"Well, we already established that you're my girlfriend. You're special to me, and I want to spend as much time as possible with you."

"I want that too, so I have an important question."

"What's that?"

"Will you be my date to my parents' tomorrow?"

"That depends. Do we have to steal glances here and there like last time? Or can I hold your hand? Can I kiss you on the cheek? Or even on the lips? Can I tell your dad his daughter is the most precious thing in the world to me?"

She didn't say a word, but Tony noticed her chest rising and falling rapidly.

"Did I scare you?"

"No."

"What are you feeling?"

"Like I wasted a lot of time, not seeing what was right in front of me."

"And what's that?"

"A man who treats me like a precious gift, who

waited for me, and who any woman would be lucky to call her boyfriend."

Things shifted between them. Tony didn't know if her emotions could ever catch up with his, but he felt …? Was it too soon to call it love?

The waitress arrived then, bringing him back to the present. He vowed not to get ahead of himself, to take every day he could spend with Anna as a blessing. They enjoyed their meal; he shared his lasagna, she shared her ravioli, and they talked about nothing and everything all at the same time. They split tiramisu for dessert and watched the sun set over the water from their table. It was a perfect day, and although he didn't want it to end, he found himself wanting to arrive back at her apartment. To walk her to the door, brush her hair aside, admire her sun-kissed skin and touch his lips to hers.

~

It was the perfect day, and although most of the ride home was spent without much conversation, it wasn't needed. They were comfortable with each other now. She felt no need to engage in those first-date rituals— because this wasn't a typical first date. They had spent so much time, first as friends, then over the last several weeks getting to know each other better. It's as if they had been dating forever, yet the butterflies were still there. Her boldness from earlier today on the water was now replaced by anticipation. She wanted Tony to kiss her when he walked her to the door, and it's all she could think of as she rested her head on his shoulder during the drive. But she didn't have to wait quite that long. He pulled in her driveway, unpacked her paddleboard, set it by her porch, then took her in his arms.

"I can't run the risk of you beating me to the punch again." Then he lowered his head to hers and kissed her, soft at first then with a little more intensity, then he pulled back and seemed to drink her in.

"Did I render you speechless?"

"You would be the first."

"Wow, I'm pretty proud of myself."

"I had an amazing time."

"So did I, and I'm already looking forward to tomorrow."

"Me too."

"Can I pick you up for church?"

"I already promised Elizabeth she could. We were going to grab coffee first. Is that okay?"

"Of course. I'm sure you are dying to tell her about the handsome man you spent the day with."

"He is pretty handsome. And thoughtful and sweet, and it's so easy to make him blush." Then she stood on her toes, brushed her lips to his cheek, and moved toward the door.

"Wow, you better not let that guy go."

"I don't plan on it," then she turned and left him staring after her, feeling his absence and counting the hours until tomorrow morning.

~

Anna finished spilling the details of her date to Elizabeth. Her friend was still grinning as she sat and finished her caramel latte and bagel.

"I'm so happy for you two. Though if you would have listened to me …"

"I know, I know, it would have happened much sooner. So, you keep telling me. But I don't care, Liz.

142

It's perfect. Maybe this is how it was all supposed to happen."

Then Elizabeth's smile slipped away, and Anna turned around and saw Garrett walking toward them like they had been friends forever.

"How are my two favorite girls?" he asked when he reached their table.

She was sure she looked dumbfounded. The audacity of the question caught her off guard and propelled her into silence.

"Oh, come on, you're not still mad at me about the competition, are you? I told you that's how guys act. Ask anyone. No one likes to lose."

Still, they said nothing. Not even Liz, who is never at a loss for words.

"Listen, I guess I should have said this sooner, but I'm sorry. Will you both forgive me?"

"Sure," said Anna, while Elizabeth just nodded her head. Maybe if they pledged their forgiveness, he would leave them alone. Anna noticed that Garrett ignored her friend and put his focus back on her. "Anna, I miss you. We had so much fun together. Will you give me another chance?"

"Why would she do that?" asked Elizabeth firmly.

"I got this, Liz. Listen, Garrett. We're over, okay? But thanks for apologizing."

"Besides, she found someone way better than you anyway."

"Liz!"

"Sorry, Anna, but this guy was a jerk to you."

"Moved on already, huh, Anna? I hope this guy can live up to your unrealistic expectations."

Did he just say that? Now she was as mad as her

friend.

"Expecting someone to treat me with respect is not unrealistic," she said calmly. "Elizabeth is right. I have moved on, but I wish you the best."

"Who is it?"

"That's none of your business."

"It's Tony, right? I saw you two all cozy after church. I knew you were a thing when you and I were together. You act all high and mighty when the whole time we were dating, you were cheating on me."

"I wasn't cheating on you. Tony and I were friends. But you know what you made me realize? That I had a great guy in front of me all along, so yes, I'm happy now. With Tony. And you should leave."

"Good for you, Anna," Elizabeth said when he walked away.

"Why did you have to goad him like that?"

"Excuse me?"

"He didn't need to know my business, Elizabeth. Sometimes you just need to stay out of it. Now he's going to be watching us at church, and it's going to be even more awkward than it already is."

"I'm sorry. You know how I get. I just can't stand that guy. Come on, let's head to church. I'll ask God's forgiveness for hurting you."

Anna shot her an eye roll, and they left. She never stayed mad at anyone but now dreaded showing up at church. Sometimes she really wished her feisty friend could show some restraint. While Elizabeth drove, Anna sent off a text to Tony. "Just had a really awkward run-in with Garrett. Elizabeth told him we are together, and now I expect things to be more awful than normal."

"What do you need?"

"Maybe lay off the hand-holding. I'm sorry. The guy just gives me the creeps, and I don't want to add fuel to the fire."

"I won't let him hurt you, Anna."

"I know."

"We can't hide forever."

"I know that too."

"I will say a prayer."

"Thank you. See you soon."

~

Anna's text stung. What did she care if Garrett saw them together? Did she still have feelings for the guy, or was she genuinely worried? He got his answer as soon as the service started, and he immediately regretted doubting her. The hatred emanated from the stage where Garrett stood singing. How could that even be possible? The guy was up there leading the praise and worship with anger in his heart. Tony stood next to Anna, yet he hadn't touched her. She was right, something was off with Garrett, and they didn't need to get him any madder than he already was. But as they sang, Tony lightly felt for her hand, as no one could see them over the pews. It was shaking. He squeezed her fingers and sent up another prayer that God would take charge of this situation.

~

A few hours later, all thoughts of Garrett were gone. Tony enjoyed hanging out with Anna's family, and today was no different. He loved the loudness, the arguing, the laughing, the teasing—he savored every second of it. Tony held Anna's hand from time to time, touched the small of her back, smiled at her all through dinner, and he knew her parents witnessed all of it, especially Helena. And he could tell they approved. And then it hit him. He wanted to be part of this family—was that a possibility? It was early in their relationship, yes, but he prayed it would happen. He took her hand again, and Christian yelled across the table. "Okay, you lovebirds. That's enough. I need some guy time. Tony, Dad, you in?"

Tony looked over at Anna, and she nodded her head. "Come on, dude, you need my sister to give you permission?"

"Hey," said Gina. "I think it's sweet. Maybe you should take a hint from him."

It was as if the air left the room. Did Gina just tell her husband to take tips from Tony, her ex-boyfriend?"

"I just meant," Gina started to stammer.

Everyone burst out laughing, releasing the tension.

"You're right, babe. I'm an idiot. May I, please go have some guy time? I will miss you like crazy."

She swatted him on the butt with the dish towel and shooed him to the other room. "Men!"

~

As soon as they were alone, her mother started in. "You are so cute together. I can tell things have really intensified between you two."

"I agree. Tell us everything."

She shared the details of her date and how much she was falling for him. When she was done, her mood changed as she thought of what happened at church that morning.

"What's wrong, Anna?" asked Gina, leaning over and placing her hand on her sister-in-law's.

Anna wore her feelings on her sleeve, so she told

them what transpired in the coffee shop. Her mother balled her fists together, gritted her teeth, and physically restrained herself from jumping up and raising hell.

"Mom, stop. You realize that if you act this way, I will keep things from you. You always say I can tell you anything, so I did."

"I know. I'm sorry. Thank you for confiding in us, Anna."

"Be careful, Anna," added Gina.

"I'm sure it will all work out. I love that church so much, and I hate that all this happened and that it's distracting me from the reason I go every week."

"I'm proud of you, Anna," said Gina.

"For what?"

"For being strong, for not backing down. And for opening your heart to Tony. I agree with your mom. You two are great together. You deserve so much happiness."

Chapter 15

Anna surveyed the scene set up in her apartment and was proud of herself. She wanted everything to be perfect. Over the last two months that she and Tony had been officially dating, she was happier than ever. They saw each other as much as possible. Every Sunday, at church, then family dinner. On Friday and Saturday and a day or two during the week. He constantly spoiled her, and today she wanted to do something special for him.

It was June now, and the Florida heat was bearing down on them, making it impossible to be outside unless they were in the water—even at night. So, she delivered the picnic to her living room. She looked at the blanket spread on the floor, daisies in the middle with an array of Italian delicacies all around it—every single item one of Tony's favorites. She secretly kept a list these past few months and made many of them today. She snapped a pic of the spread and sent it off to Grace, Gina, and Elizabeth, who replied first: "Can I be your boyfriend?"

"LOL, Liz," Grace chimed back. "That looks amazing, Anna, have a wonderful time."

"I want all the details tomorrow," said Gina.

She told her friends goodbye, then Anna received a personal message from Gina. "Remember what we talked about, Anna. Don't be afraid. God will tell you what to do. Just tell Tony how you feel."

"Thanks, G."

She placed her phone on the counter and considered Gina's comment. Anna confided in her the other day that she loved Tony and wanted to tell him but fear stopped her. Gina insisted there was nothing to worry about. That it was apparent Tony loved her too—he would be thrilled that she returned the sentiment. He was waiting to make sure Anna was ready.

Anna looked at her watch again and waited, eager to see the surprise on Tony's handsome face. He thought they were staying in, ordering takeout, and watching a movie. She heard a knock and immediately opened it without hesitation. But it wasn't Tony who entered her apartment and closed the door behind her.

A few hours earlier

Garrett stood at the podium, trying to pretend he was happy with second place—again. He was failing miserably. After winning his past few competitions, something about being here in this spot brought everything from that day with Anna and Elizabeth flooding back. Things had been fine with him and Anna until then. They probably would still be together if it wasn't for blondie putting all those negative ideas in Anna's head. She would still be with him instead of Saint Tony, king of the baseball team and hero of Tarpon High.

He left the competition, went home, and had a few beers but still was in a foul mood. It had done nothing to calm him down. He grabbed his keys and took off toward his car.

~

"Garrett, what are you doing here?" said Anna. "You really need to leave," but he pushed his way inside and shut the door.

"Come on, Anna, give me another chance," he said. She could smell the alcohol on his breath, and fear began to well up inside her. Her eyes darted to the closed door now blocked by his massive body. His muscles no longer held appeal. All she saw now was the damage he could cause with his brute strength. He moved closer, and she tried not to cower in fear, though she never felt more terrified.

~

"We've talked about this. Please leave me alone. I hope you find someone who makes you happy, but it's not me."

"Why not, baby? Remember the fun we had that day when you blew off your family?"

"I'm not your baby, and I'm not the girl who blows people off. Please go." Her eyes scanned the room again, knowing there was still no escape but foolishly hoping one had miraculously appeared.

His face changed before her. He was done playing nice, and her heartbeat accelerated. The sweat started to bead on her forehead, and her palms were slippery. Where was Tony? Garrett suddenly noticed her picnic set up, and she hoped that didn't set him off further, but it was too late.

"Is Mr. Baseball Hero coming over? Why did you never do anything like this for me, Anna?"

"Because I don't feel the same way about you as I do about Tony. I'm sorry, I really hope you find someone ..."

He cut her off and grabbed her wrist hard. The pain sliced through her wrist and took off all the way to her shoulder. Although she tried to scream, no sounds emerged from her mouth.

"Listen, Anna. I tried to be nice about this, but you can't just screw around with people's feelings."

"I didn't ..."

"Shut up. I'm not done." Then he shoved her into the wall, and she landed in a heap on the floor. Her thin frame still landed with a thud due to the sheer force that sent her reeling. Anna's hands trembled furiously. She held them together to stop the pulsating, but it was no use. Her shoulder and wrist throbbed with pain from hitting the wall then the hard floor.

"And don't even think about reporting this to anyone. No one will believe you. You're the one who will come out scarred if you even try to take me down."

Take him down? What was happening? She couldn't see straight. Her tears blocked her vision, but she refused to let them fall down her face. She didn't want him to hear her sob. He paced back and forth across her living room a few times as if to figure out his next move, then he slammed the door and was gone.

Tony took the steps up to Anna's apartment two at a time. He couldn't wait to see her and express how much he loved her, as he wasn't able to hold it in any longer. He knocked on her door, but no one answered, and was about to rap harder when he heard the sobs.

"Anna, what's going on? Answer the door."

The sounds got louder, but there was no sign of Anna.

"Anna, you're scaring me. If you don't open the

door, I swear I will break it down."

It sounded like someone was crawling toward the door, then he heard the lock turn, and the door was open, but still, she didn't appear. He pushed it open with force and saw her huddled in a ball on the floor, holding her arm and wincing. He closed the gap between them in less than a second.

"Anna, what happened?"

When she didn't answer him or even move, he pulled her close, and her cries became even louder. He held her while taking in the room--the picnic blanket, the flowers, an array of gourmet food. Did she do all this for him? And what happened before he arrived?

"Anna, you're scaring me. Please tell me what happened!"

"Garrett was here."

"Did he touch you? I'll kill him." Apparently, that got her attention, and she jerked her head up and tried to squirm out of his embrace. "No, you can't say a word!"

"Why not? You have to tell me everything, Anna."

The story came out in fits and starts, and Tony stroked her hair, vowing he would take care of her.

"I love you, Anna. I planned on telling you that tonight. I didn't think it would happen like this, but I love you and will protect you."

"But you didn't, did you?" she lashed out, surprising him.

"Where were you? Why weren't you here?"

"Anna, I was here right on time. How could I have known? I'm so sorry. But I will fix this."

"You won't! I told you what he said. No one will believe me, and he's right."

"Anna!"

"I'm serious, Tony. You can't say a word."

He lay her on the couch, covered her up with a blanket, and whispered for her to rest. He kissed her on the forehead, then started to clean up all the food.

"I did that for you. I made all your favorites. I'm sorry the night was ruined. That everything is ruined."

He practically ran back to where she lay on the couch. "Listen to me, that's not true. We will get past this. You did nothing wrong here. You know that, right?"

The stillness was his answer, and hopelessness engulfed him. He looked to the couch and could already see Anna's eyes drooping, her river of tears finally tiring her out. He texted Gina and Christian and apologized but asked if they could find someone to watch the kids and come over. He didn't want to scare them but told them it was urgent and not to tell anyone where they were going. "Be there in 30 minutes. But you're scaring us," said Gina. He didn't try to alleviate her fears. How could he when the demons were right at his door.

Tony stood at the window waiting for his friends to arrive while glancing back at Anna to ensure she was still sleeping. When he saw their car pull up, he tiptoed outside and prayed she wouldn't stir. He relayed the whole story while Gina started crying. Christian clenched his fists, vowing to kill Garrett, just as Tony had done a few hours before.

"We have to call Pastor Tom," said Gina. "He loves Anna. He has known all of us way longer than Garrett. He married us."

"I agree, but you didn't see her, Gina. She became

more visibly upset when I talked about going to the church."

"You have to," said Christian. "If you don't, I will."

"Do I call him now? Do I send you guys away? Do I stay until she wakes up? I don't know what to do. I thought it would help if she woke up to have you both here but now, I don't know."

"Go make the call," said Gina. "He can't get away with this. Garrett works at the church. He leads the praise and worship. We would be doing the church a disservice if we didn't say anything."

"I agree with you," Tony said while rubbing his hand through his hair. "But you didn't see her."

"Do you love my sister?" Christian asked.

"With all my heart."

Gina's gaze dropped to her feet.

"What?" Tony asked.

"She loves you back. She wanted to tell you that tonight."

Tony kicked a piece of gravel on the driveway. "I'll kill that guy for ruining this."

"That will only happen if you let him," said Gina. "Now make that call and take care of your girl."

"Thanks, Gina."

"No problem. We'll tiptoe inside in case Anna wakes up. You better do it out here, so she doesn't hear you."

~

Tony got off the phone with Pastor Tom, and the peace he prayed for never came. The pastor calmly listened to Tony's words, asked how Anna was doing, and it was evident he was concerned. But the urgency that Anna deserved was nowhere to be found. When she woke up, Tony wanted to tell her that it was taken care of and that everything would be okay. That she would never have to see Garrett again, and everything would go back to normal. He knew it was a dream. When they ended the call, Pastor Tom promised to investigate the situation and get back to him. The conversation did nothing to calm his fears. Restlessness overpowered him. What would Anna do when she found out he broke her trust? Would they be over before they barely began? He put that scenario out of his head and prayed. "Dear Lord, please protect this woman I love so much. Take control of this situation as only You can do." Then he entered the house, not knowing what he was walking into. It was worse than he thought.

She looked up at him from the couch, her face stained with fresh tears. Gina sat on one side of her and Christian on the other.

"I trusted you."

She said it so quietly, he almost didn't hear her.

"Anna," Gina started.

"Don't."

"Don't what, sis?" yelled Christian, jumping off the couch. "Don't care about you? Just let this guy who shoved you and dishonored you with his words walk around and do this to others? I thought you were stronger than this."

It was so quiet you could hear faint rustling outside. Inside it was eerily still.

"Apparently, you were wrong. I'm not cut out to handle any of this. And where are your kids? If you told mom, I will never talk to either of you again."

"Give us some credit, Anna. We told mom we needed an impromptu night out. She knows nothing."

"It better stay that way."

"It will," they all said in unison.

She looked right at Tony. "You've said that before. You lost my trust."

"Anna, I know you're hurting," said Gina. "But Tony doesn't deserve this. You can't expect him to ignore this."

"I told him not to call Pastor Tom, and he did." She turned to him now. "So, you may as well spit it out. What did he say?"

"He's looking into the situation."

"I have a bad feeling about this."

Christian sat down next to her again. "Why, sis?"

"You see Garrett at church. He looks like the perfect vision of godliness up there. All this stuff we see no one else does. They are going to call me a liar. I know it."

"I think you're wrong. People can discern these things. I don't think you're the only one."

"I hope you're right."

Anna's phone went off on the counter, indicating a text message. Gina picked up the device and handed it to her. The blood drained from Anna's face leaving a ghost color in its wake. The sobs wrecked her again, so Gina held her close and stroked her hair while Christian read the messages.

"I'll kill him," he said, then handed the phone to Tony. Once he read them, he looked at Anna with so much sorrow and apologies.

"Look what you've done," she said.

"Will someone please tell me what's going on?" Gina pleaded.

Tony summarized the messages. "Garrett sent her a

text asking her why she was lying. He talks like a saint and asks why she is accusing him of things he didn't do. He's setting up his case. He's acting like this never happened."

Tony's gaze moved to the woman he loved so much, her eyes blood-red, and his heart broke into a few more pieces. He couldn't stand seeing her like this and not being able to comfort her. He wondered then if he did ruin everything. He looked over at her. She met his eyes and said, "I think you should go."

"Anna," Gina started.

"Stay out of this, Gina."

Christian stepped forward and draped his arm around his wife. "We better get back before mom gets suspicious. She knows we don't stay out this late," he joked, trying to get a laugh from his sister. It didn't appear that she registered what he said. Tony wondered what she was thinking but didn't want to know all at the same time.

Gina knelt, so she was at eye level with Anna. "I'll be back in the morning."

"You don't have to."

"She'll be here, Anna. Stop arguing," said her brother.

They said goodbye, and Anna leveled her gaze at Tony. "You need to leave too."

"I'm sorry, but I can't."

She didn't argue even though Tony knew she was furious with him. Which only meant she was scared to be alone.

"Have you eaten anything today?"

"Not since lunch."

"Do you want me to get you anything?"

"No, but help yourself, and when you leave, take it with you. I made it all for you anyway."

"I'm sorry, Anna."

"I assume you're staying on the couch?" though she didn't wait for him to answer. "Everything you need is in the linen closet in the hallway."

"Thank you."

Then she turned and walked away, and Tony wondered how this night filled with promise turned into the worst of his life.

~

Tony greeted Gina the following day, and it was clear she was surprised to see him there.

"I slept on the couch," he explained. "I wasn't going to leave her alone, Gina."

"I'm glad you stayed. Anna needs you."

"She won't talk to me."

"I'm so sorry, Tony. I know how much you care about her."

Tony ran his fingers through his hair, lost in thought.

"This is the first time I have had such strong feelings for someone since..."

"Since me, I know."

Tony knew this went way beyond what he and Gina had, and he remembered how distraught he was when they broke up, as fleeting as their relationship was. How would he get over losing Anna? He couldn't even think that way. The awkwardness was broken by the sound of his phone buzzing.

"It's Liz. She wants to know why no one is at church today."

"Tell her it's too long to text, and you will call her

later."

"Done," then his phone pinged again, and Tony's face fell.

"What?"

Tony read the text. "Garrett keeps looking at me and is as smug as ever. It's weird."

"Call me right after church, and I'll fill you in," he texted back to her.

"Do you think it's odd that you haven't heard back from the pastor yet?" Gina asked.

"Not really. It's Sunday, he will be at church most of the day. But if I don't hear back by tonight, I'm calling him."

"What do I tell Helena about dinner? Christian thinks we should tell her Anna is sick."

"I think he is right. It's best to not say anything until we hear from the pastor."

"You know we can't hold off Helena forever."

"I know. I just pray it won't be for that long."

"Don't take this the wrong way, but you look like crud."

Tony smiled at her, thankful they were now friends.

"Why don't you go home and rest? I will tell Anna you were here."

"Do you think she will forgive me, Gina?"

"There is nothing to forgive. She is going through a rough time. I will help her through this."

"Thanks, Gina. Please tell her ..."

"I will."

~

When the sound of the doorbell interrupted his frantic thoughts, he opened it quickly, knowing exactly who would be standing on the other side.

"I know something is going on, Tony. Tell me."

After divulging all that transpired in the past 18 hours, he watched Elizabeth's body rise and fall as the sobs poured out. Exhaustion finally claimed him, and although his heart ached for her, he had nothing left to give. How could he continue to console other people when his heart was shattering?

The soft hand on his back was a reprieve from the harshness of the day.

"I'm so sorry, Tony. I know how much you love her." He lifted his eyes to meet hers, and they were full of questions.

"Please. I know you too well. Anyway, I'm sorry I'm making you take care of me when you are so worried about Anna."

"It's fine, Elizabeth, but you have to promise me you won't confront him."

"I won't."

Her easy answer stunned him.

"I'm scared of him now."

Elizabeth, the strong, spunky one, was scared. This guy was not going to win. Tony vowed to protect the women in his life, but he couldn't do it alone. So he bowed his head and prayed some more.

~

Tony paced his living room for the millionth time that day when his phone finally rang, and the name he was waiting to see lit up the screen. Anticipation, and at the same time dread, filled him.

"Pastor Tom."

"Hi, Tony. How's Anna?"

"Not good."

"I noticed none of you were in church today."

Tony was taken aback by the tactlessness in that statement from a man he respected—until now. The pastor must have noticed it from his silence.

"I'm sorry, that was insensitive of me."

"She's not good at all. We know Garrett was in church today, so why don't you tell me what's going on?"

"He said she's lying."

"And you believe him?"

"My hands are tied."

Tony attempted to gain his composure before he answered, but those efforts were futile.

"How exactly are your hands tied? You are choosing to believe him over her, case closed?"

"That's all I can do for now."

"For now? So, you're just waiting until he hurts someone else, and you're allowing him to stand up there every Sunday acting like the perfect man of God that people look up to?"

"I'm sorry."

"And you wonder why people are losing faith in the church. This isn't over," and he hung up.

Tony had grown up in the church and always possessed a deep faith in God. But at this moment, that was being severely tested. How was he going to explain this to Anna? He didn't have long to think about that when his phone rang. She ignored his texts all day, so he was relieved she was calling but also afraid of the words he would hear. Of the questions, she would ask and the answers he would be forced to give.

"I'm glad you called," he said. "How are you?"

"The same. What did the pastor say?"

"I just got off the phone and was going to call you."

"It's bad, isn't it?"

"It is. I'm so sorry. He said his hands are tied."

Her cries reverberated through the phone. He waited for her to take a breath.

"Thanks for calling off Elizabeth."

A laugh escaped his mouth unexpectedly and gave him hope that the same Anna was still in there. That she would recover from this and be okay.

"You're welcome. I would do anything for you."

"I know, but I need time."

"I'm here. You know that, right? I'm always here."

He wasn't surprised at her silence, so he plowed ahead, wanting to get this next part over.

"You have to call the pastor, Anna."

"It won't make a difference."

"It will. He has to hear from you what happened. You can't just let this go."

"Good night, Tony."

He stared at his phone, contemplating how this had all gone so terribly wrong. Why was God deserting him now that he was finally happy and looking forward to a promising future with a woman he loved? Why was He hurting such a beautiful woman who was growing closer to him with every passing day?

Chapter 16

A week passed since the incident, and Anna couldn't hold off her mother any longer. Even her dad was calling and texting more than usual. Last week Christian told the family she was sick, but she had to show up at Sunday dinner today. Gina and Christian said they would be there when she told her story, but she knew it would be awful. Her parents had no idea what they were in for. They figured she and Tony broke up, which was true, but they thought that was where the story ended. They had no idea what else Anna endured. She called in sick on Monday but somehow muddled through the rest of the week. Anna knew her boss sensed something was wrong by the easy stories she was assigned, which was a departure from the types of articles she usually wrote.

She grabbed her purse and shut the door, dreading the moment ahead but wanting to get it over with so she could retreat back to her bed and huddle in a ball under the covers. Her brother's car was parked in the drive, which gave her some level of comfort as she didn't want to face her parents alone.

Her mother opened the door before Anna knocked and pulled her into her arms. Her dad walked out and embraced her as well but not before shooting her mother a concerned look.

"Where's everyone?"

"Gina and Christian are in the kitchen waiting for you. Eva is sleeping, and AJ is watching a movie," her mother answered.

"Let's go join them, and I will tell you what's going on."

Anna relayed her story, aware there was no emotion in her voice. She knew her mother was shaken, and that wasn't an easy thing to do.

"I thought ..."

"I know. You and Dad figured Tony and I broke up, and you wanted to give me space."

"If I had known, Anna."

"Stop, I didn't want to talk about it, and I still don't. You both deserve to know, but that's it. I want to move on."

Her mother opened her mouth, but her father reached across the table and held her hand, signaling to let him speak.

"Is this what moving on looks like, Anna? Your face is pale, there are bags under your eyes, and it looks like you already shed some pounds. I'm worried about you. Now is not the time to be turning people away. Especially that boyfriend of yours."

"That boyfriend of mine—ex, by the way—made things worse by going to the church."

"How could you think that?" her father yelled. "I would have laid into him if he didn't speak out. You can't let Garrett get away with this."

"Watch me. And you're right, Dad, I have lost weight because I'm not eating. Enjoy your dinner." Then she picked up her purse and left.

~

A few hours later, she received a text from Gina. "I'm at your door."

Anna let her in but returned to her spot on the couch. "Come on, Anna. Your mom sent food. You have to eat something."

"I'm not hungry."

"If you don't, I'll sic your mother on you."

"It's Dad who scared me today. Talk about a change in roles," she said, walking over to the kitchen where Gina was fixing her a plate. "Give it to me straight. How bad is it?"

"It's not good. I think they plan on calling Tony."

"Great, they can all conspire against me."

"No one is doing that, Anna. But I know what you're going through, so I'm here for you. And everyone seemed to agree I'm the only one you may talk to right now."

"I know it's only been a week, and you went through so much more than I did, and it was so much worse, but ..."

"First of all, stop. You lost your brother and your niece."

"But I had my family to support me. We all deserted you."

"You were one of the first ones to come back to me, Anna. And yes, I know what you are going through. I know what it's like to be so far down in the pit of despair that you think you will never crawl out. So, I'm here for you."

"It's hard to breathe. I look at that food, and I can't eat. I can't sleep because I see Garrett shoving me even in my dreams. I miss Tony so much it hurts, but I also blame him for what he did. I have so much anger and don't know what to do with it."

Anna inhaled and plunged on. "I also have a lot of guilt about you."

"Me?"

"I've been curled up in a ball all week, and my phone has been blowing up with people checking on me. I can't stop thinking about how we left you alone after Alex and Teresa died, and the guilt just knocks me over."

"You have to let that go, Anna. I don't blame you for any of that."

Anna stuffed the rest of her worries deep down. She knew Gina may still be dealing with the effects of postpartum depression. Gina was not the person Anna should be pouring her heart out to. Why then did she sense that Gina could be the only one who could help her?

Gina placed a small plate in front of her.

"Please just take a few bites so I can tell your mother you ate something."

"Fine." She chewed in silence, wanting to ask if Gina had talked to Tony, but restrained herself.

"Tony wanted me to tell you he misses you."

Anna missed everything about him but took a few more mouthfuls without saying a word.

"He also wanted me to tell you he prays every day that God will bring you through this and that you will forgive him for hurting you."

Anna pushed the plate away, dropped the fork, and the sobs once again consumed her. Gina pulled her close but not before Anna saw the look of guilt in her eyes.

"I'm sorry, Anna. I didn't mean to upset you more."

"You didn't, Gina. I miss him. But everything is so messed up. And please don't say it."

"Say what?" she asked, feigning ignorance. "That God has a plan? Oh, thanks for mentioning it because He does."

Anna smiled. "I love you, Gina. Thanks for being here for me, even though I didn't do the same for you."

"You need to stop saying that, Anna. The past is over. We're family, and family looks out for one another."

Anna watched Gina's face fall as she realized what she said, knowing she wanted to take it back but couldn't.

"Exactly, family is there for each other. And I wasn't there for you. And now that I'm in this hole, which is only a small one compared to the ditch you were in, I realize how much I let you down. Maybe God is punishing for me that."

"He's not punishing you, Anna. God doesn't work like that. I have forgiven you, and you must forgive yourself. And don't let what that jerk Garrett did have power over you. You are so much stronger than this."

Then why did the desire to crawl under the covers and block the world out forever engulf her?

~

Two weeks passed since Anna shut Tony out. When he looked out the window at the two people coming up the walk, he found himself surprised they stayed away this long.

"Helena, John. Come in. I know why you're here, but I don't think I can help you. Elizabeth and Gina give me updates, and Anna still doesn't want to talk to me. I can't force her."

167

"We know that, son," said John, "but we don't know what to do."

"How bad is it?"

Helena started crying, which rocked him. She never showed any emotions and was always stoic and controlled.

"It's bad," John answered for his wife. Tony noticed the way his brow furrowed, the way he touched his wife's hand, and shifted in his seat that he wasn't exaggerating. Now Tony was anxious because John was a cop. He imagined it took a lot to work him up.

"I'm sorry, but I still think I did the right thing by calling the pastor."

John jumped up from his chair. "Of course you did. The only reason I haven't gone over there is we think that will make it worse. Anna is the one who needs to tell him what happened. We can't fight this battle for her. I can't believe he didn't investigate this further, but the only way the truth will come out is if Anna speaks up."

Tony turned toward Helena, knowing John was right but surprised his wife concurred. She nodded her head, agreeing with Tony's unspoken question.

"My daughter is the strongest person in this family. She takes after her dad. I just pray that her fiery tenacity comes back once more time has passed."

Anna's parents then inquired about Tony, and he glossed over it all, saying he missed Anna but was hanging in there. He didn't mention that he couldn't sleep because the ache in his heart hurt so much. That he wonders why this happened just when they were about to declare their love. That his students noticed how despondent he is at school every day and don't know how to help.

Tony sensed there was more when John and Helena made no moves toward the door.

"What aren't you telling me?"

"She is pretty depressed. Gina told us that all this with Garrett is making her realize how awful she treated Gina after Alex and Teresa died—we all did. And now she is using what Garrett did as an excuse to relive all that guilt. She has all this self-loathing, and we are worried about her," said Helena.

"I wish I could help, but I don't know what else to do when she is ignoring me."

"We know," said John. "We just came to ask you not to give up on our daughter. She loves you, and you may be the only person who can bring her back to us. Well, you and Gina maybe."

"I have no plans on giving up on her, Sir. I pray for her every day. We are meant to be together. That's the one thing I am sure of."

Tony watched them leave, then picked up his phone to call Anna. He knew she wouldn't answer, but he had to hear her voice, even if it was her voicemail.

"Hey, Anna. I said my prayer for you this morning. I pray for you, for us, multiple times, you know. I miss talking to you, your laugh, your smile, but mostly I'm just so very sorry that you lost your joy. But you'll get it back—that I know. I love you, Anna. Remember, God's got you."

~

Anna listened to the message and hit save, along with all the others. Every day she listened to each one. She loved him but couldn't trust him. She knew he thought he did the right thing, but he hurt her in the

169

process. And that joy he mentioned—Garrett stole that from her, but Tony took some of it too, and she wasn't sure it would come back anytime soon, if ever.

~

Tony walked out to his garage to throw a Coke can in the recycling container and spotted his paddleboard leaning against the wall. He didn't want to go without Anna but had to get out of the house. To try to get his mind off her, even though he knew that was impossible. It would be even worse out on the water, which is where they had some of their best conversations. He imagined her then on her paddleboard, her sun-kissed skin glowing darker under the sun's heat, and her smile. That's what he missed most.

An hour later, Tony pulled into the lot, and there she was. He could tell she had just finished boarding—her skin was wet, and so was her paddleboard, which she was pushing into the back of her car when he arrived. Tony pulled up next to her, and she didn't even glance his way. He opened his door, and she finally looked up and saw him.

"Hey, Anna."

"I guess we had the same idea."

"We did. How is out there today?"

"Good."

"How are you?"

"I'm fine."

Anna would always be beautiful to him, but she looked anything but fine. Her natural glow was gone. It was odd to be staring at her and not seeing that signature glint in her eyes. He refused to think he was the reason for its absence. His anger welled up against Garrett again for what he stole from her—from them.

"I miss you. Have you been listening to my messages?"

She averted her eyes, and Tony's anger for Garrett built up even further. She couldn't even look at him now. A month ago, they were about to begin their love story, and now here they were acting like strangers.

"I have," were her only words as she went back to maneuvering her board in the back of her car. Tony went over to help, and she moved away immediately after their arms grazed against one another. Could she really not be around him at all?

She shut the trunk and walked to the driver's side. "Thanks for your help," then she drove away.

Tony watched her leave, and at that moment, questioned everything about their friendship, their relationship. Maybe she didn't return his feelings. Their encounter barely phased her while it shook Tony to his core. Seeing her made the ache in his heart intensify, and it hurt to see Anna's indifference to him. He opened his car door, suddenly not wanting to be in the water—near anything that reminded him of Anna and what he lost.

Anna drove away while looking through her rearview mirror until Tony's figure faded from her view. Seeing him today almost ripped her in two. She touched the place where their arms had brushed briefly, and she erupted in tears. She wished she could have spoken to Tony but knew if she did, this is what would have happened—she would have turned into a blubbering mess. So, she stood silent, didn't mention how much those heartfelt messages meant to her, that she listened to them before she went to bed each night, and sometimes multiple times in a day. She hated herself even more for what she had done to him. The Tony she saw today wasn't the man she knew. When she ignored him, his dejected expression was something she would regret but couldn't take back. She still blamed him for ruining what they had.

Anna had to pull herself together. She had ignored the family dinners for a month now, and her mother bluntly told her she expected her there today. Maybe she could have made it if she hadn't seen Tony. But now that she did, she wanted to run back to her cocoon and shut the world out once again. She sent her mom a text, told her she couldn't make it and pleaded with her to give her more time to heal. She knew her mother wouldn't listen, but she didn't care. She walked inside, took a long hot shower, shut off her phone, and climbed into bed.

~

Gina, Christian, and the kids were hanging out in the Andros' spacious kitchen when Helena saw the text.

"She canceled again. John, you need to go over there and get her."

Gina was aware that John seemed to be considering it and knew she needed to intercede.

"I know you all don't want to hear this, but I think you need to give her time. It's Anna. She's not going to stay away forever. She still needs to work through some stuff, and you pushing her isn't going to help."

"But we can't just leave her there in that house all alone and depressed," John answered.

Christian grabbed his wife's hand under the table and squeezed. Gina knew exactly what he thought when he made that gesture. While they all wanted to rush to help Anna in her depression, they did the exact opposite for Gina after Alex and Teresa died. They all just left her to languish in her grief. They were past that now, but her husband knew it still hurt at times, and this was one of them.

"Where did AJ go?" asked Christian. "Gina, let's go take him outside to play and let my parents talk."

"But you two should be here for this," said Helena. "We need to figure out what to do about Anna."

"No, Mom, I don't think you need us for that."

They turned the corner and into the hallway, and Gina fell into her husband's arms. "Thank you."

"You're welcome. I'm sorry. You know my mother is clueless sometimes. She loves you."

"I know, but thanks for saving me."

"Always."

Chapter 17

Tony walked up to his apartment, reeling from the day and eager to put its events behind him. A month ago, he was looking forward to spending the summer with Anna—surprising her at work and taking her to lunch. Picking her up and spending time on the water. But none of that was happening now, and in Anna's mind, that was all his fault. Lately, Tony was starting to question if she was right. He still reeled that Garrett was emerging unscathed while his actions unleashed severe repercussions all around him. But even worse than that, Tony wondered why Pastor Tom took Garrett's words at face value and looked no further. The system failed Anna, and Tony felt compelled to rectify the damage inflicted upon her. It couldn't get any worse. She was already ignoring him, so he formulated a plan of action.

The next night Tony showed up at the singles group, and it was worth it just to see the brief hint of fear on Garrett's smug face when he spotted Tony.

"Tony, long time, no see," said Erica, the group leader and a staple at their Sunday lunches, back when he attended those. "We were just talking about where you guys have been. Where are Anna and Elizabeth?"

"They can't make it," he said, eyeing Garrett the

whole time.

"Why not? We know how much they love it. I texted them both but never heard back. I keep meaning to give them a call."

"You should do that," said Tony. "Maybe they will open up to you about why they haven't been coming." Tony was confident he was getting under Garrett's skin and reveled in it.

Erica raised her eyebrows at his comment. "You and I will have to talk later," she said. "It sounds like there is something you aren't telling me."

"Looking forward to it," said Tony. "Let's go for coffee after."

Tony was laying it on thick and could practically see Garrett's chest rising and falling, indicating his anger. Good. Tony was getting to him. This was all part of his plan to draw him out.

After the meeting ended, Erica walked over. Tony noticed Garrett's eyes bore into him as he attempted to intimidate him.

"Ready to get that coffee?"

"Sure, let's go."

"Won't your girlfriend mind you going out with another girl? Or maybe she's not your girl anymore?" Garrett said with an edge.

"Oh, she is, and she doesn't mind. I would never jeopardize what we have. I would do anything for Anna." It wasn't exactly a lie, Tony reasoned. She was his girl, and he would make sure Anna knew how much he loved her and that he would move mountains to protect her.

For the first time that night, Garrett's gaze dropped slightly to the floor, perhaps signifying he sensed what

Tony was implying.

As soon as they were out of earshot, Erica started in.

"Yikes, I thought I was going to have to send you two outside to settle the girlfriend score."

He studied her, trying to decipher from her expression how much she knew. He didn't have to wait long.

"Oh, come on, everyone knows those two were dating, then all of a sudden, you and Anna went from friends to a serious relationship. We're all surprised it took this long for you all to face each other."

"So, people are talking about us?"

"Only to say we figured why none of you come to the group anymore. We determined it had to be the awkwardness of the situation."

He breathed a sigh of relief, glad to know no one else realized what transpired. He didn't need Anna to be at the forefront of gossip, which would upset her even more.

"What else is going on?"

"Nothing. I just miss you guys. I figured I would see how Garrett reacted to me first before Anna came back," he lied.

"We miss you too. Things have been weird lately."

"In what way?"

"It's different without you, Elizabeth, and Anna. And Garrett's all moody. I thought he just missed Anna. No offense, the guy can get any girl. So, I'm starting to think it's more than that."

Tony kept his words at bay. That Anna was a treasure and not just any girl for Garrett to conquer.

"Any ideas?"

"No, but he wasn't happy to see you, that was clear. Maybe he is just jealous. I hope you all can work it out eventually. I miss us all hanging out."

"Me too."

"Can I ask you a question?"

"Sure."

"I understand you guys not wanting to come to small group to face Garrett in such close quarters. But what about church? You three attended every Sunday."

Tony tried to figure out how to explain it. He refused to reveal that the thought of seeing Garrett act all pious up on stage turned his stomach to knots. Or that hearing Pastor Tom talk about caring for others would make him want to run screaming from the sanctuary. So, he said it was a difficult time for them all, and the situation would work itself out soon. Another lie. He wondered why he met Erica. Did he really think she was going to come out with all these seedy stories about Garrett? And how was he supposed to find out if she knew anything? He was so desperate to fix his relationship with Anna that he was grasping. But he also was sure that Garrett had a history, and he needed to uncover it to get Pastor Tom to see the light. He wanted Anna to feel safe and hopefully forgive him.

"Tony?"

He heard Erica say his name and wondered how long he ignored her.

"Sorry, I was just thinking."

"About Anna?"

"Yes."

"Is everything really okay with her?"

"Yes, it's fine, don't worry."

"You're a great guy, Tony. Tell Anna I hope to see

her soon and that I am praying for her."

"I will."

~

Garrett sat outside Anna's apartment, contemplating his next move. He didn't need Tony going around asking questions about him and for people to start gossiping. Garrett liked it at First United. He earned a small stipend for leading the worship team each Sunday, and it helped him pay for his competitions. There was no way Garrett would allow Tony to mess that up. Or Anna. If she had just stayed with him, none of this would have happened. It was time to send her another message, so he opened the car door, walked up, and knocked.

Anna peeked through the window, saw Garrett's car, and immediately started to shiver. The fear pulsated through her body, causing her hands and legs to shake. Her phone was across the room, but she didn't want to risk getting it and having him hear her. She wished it was nearby so she could hit record and have some proof of Garrett's vile actions.

"Anna, I know you're in there. I'm only here to send you a little warning. Call off your boyfriend, or you'll be sorry." She heard him walk down the steps in a hurry, then looked through the curtain again and saw his BMW headed down the street. Her hands were still shaking and her heart pounding. Was she always going to have to live in fear of him? She strode across the room in anger, picked up her phone, and hit Tony's number.

"Hey, Anna, it's nice to hear from you."

"What did you do?"

"What do you mean?"

"Garrett was here."

"Did he hurt you again?"

Anna caught the anger in his voice but couldn't allow it to get to her. To allow him to be her protector.

"No, but you did." Her voice was devoid of emotion when she said it.

"How did I hurt you? I love you, Anna. I'm trying to protect you from him. All I did was go to the small group. I just wanted to make him squirm. That's it. To let him know I'm watching him."

"Well, I don't think it worked. Because Garrett was cocky enough to come over, knock on my door like it was the most normal thing in the world and tell me I better call you off or I would be sorry."

She heard his breath catch, but she balled her fists together and vowed not to allow her emotions to overtake her.

"I'm coming over. I miss you so much it hurts. I just need to see your face."

"I didn't answer for him, and I won't for you either. Let me go, Tony."

~

Garrett sat in his car parked outside his second house of the night. He knew he would have to turn on the charm for this one, so he stole a look in the rearview mirror, practiced his signature smile that made women swoon, and headed toward the door.

"Hey Garrett, what are you doing here?" asked Erica. "It's late."

"I know, sorry. But you told me you are a night owl, so I figured I would take a chance and stop by."

She looked at her watch for the second time since she opened the door.

"It's 10:00."

"I'm sorry. I should go. I'll come back tomorrow."

He turned to leave, heard her call his name, and the smile played on his lips. "Every time," he thought as he turned back toward the house.

"It's not that important. I just really wanted someone to talk to. I was going to ask you to hang out after group, but then I heard you and Tony make plans for coffee, and I didn't want to intrude."

"That was probably a good idea," she said while gesturing for him to follow her inside.

"Why's that?"

"Drop the act, Garrett. I thought I was going to have to send you two outside to settle the score."

"There is no score."

"You could have fooled me. I figured you were mad because Tony got the girl we all know you wanted."

He tried to pretend he didn't care. He clenched his fists, digging his nails into his hands, and swore he drew blood.

"They aren't together anymore. Tony didn't win."

"Well, then why did you look like you want to kill him? Neither of you is with her, so why the venomous looks all night?"

"I'm worried about Anna."

"Try again."

Maybe he shouldn't have come here. He forgot for a second how perceptive Erica was.

"Fine, I want her back. But I don't think she is emotionally stable. I need her to take care of herself. I'm upset with Tony because he won't leave her alone and give her space."

She studied him long and hard, and he wondered if

she was buying it. Then she lifted her hand and put it on his.

"I think you might be wrong. I have known those two for a while, and I always wondered why they weren't more than friends. I'm sorry if this hurts you, but I sense they have a real bond."

"She's not going to get better if he is always hanging around."

"I think you're wrong, but I'll talk to him."

"No, I don't want you to do that for me."

"Stop, I want to. I care about you."

He smiled in the knowledge that his plan worked. He suspected Erica had feelings for him. He just had to nudge those to the surface and tug on her heartstrings. He was going to come out of this smelling like a bed of roses.

~

When his classes were over for the day, Tony picked up his phone and was surprised to see a message from Erica. "Can we meet for coffee again?"

That was odd. Why did she want to see him again? He thought back to everything he said the night before. Did he send her mixed signals? Did she think he was interested in her? How could she when he told her how he felt about Anna? His mind was racing, and he was sure he was overreacting, so he texted back, "Sure."

~

For the second night in a row, Tony sat at a coffee shop across from Erica. He studied her as she kneaded her hands together nervously. Oh man, maybe she really did like him and thought this was some sort of date? How was his life getting so confusing? Thankfully, Erica finally broke the silence.

"So, Garrett came by last night."

He immediately tensed. It must have been pretty late. What was with this guy? What was he trying to prove?

"Yeah, what, is he after you now?"

"Tony! Would that be such a bad thing?"

"Erica, you just told me last night you thought he was acting strange, and now you report he shows up at your house unannounced. What's going on, and what do I have to do with it?"

"He's worried about Anna, and now I am too."

"Listen to me, Erica. That guy is bad news, and you can't believe a word that comes out of his mouth. Stay away from him."

"Or what?"

"Or you may get hurt just like Anna did, but this time it could be worse."

"Listen, Tony, I don't know what your problem is, but you can't go around making threats like that. It's creepy."

"I'm not the one you need to be worried about. Stay away from Garrett." Then he walked away, realizing this guy was considerably more dangerous than he thought.

Chapter 18

Gina opened the door to welcome Grace and Elizabeth into her home. They had barely entered before AJ came barreling down the hallway enveloping Liz in one of his monster hugs. Gina giggled inwardly as Grace pretended to cry, knowing her sweet boy would come to the rescue.

"Miss Grace, why are you crying?"

"Because you didn't give me a hug," but she couldn't help breaking into a wide smile.

"Here's your hug! I saved the biggest one just for you."

"Hey! I thought I was your favorite," teased Liz.

"I love you both equal," he said while grabbing Grace with one hand and Liz with the other. "Let's go see sissy. But shh, she's sleeping."

AJ led the women over to where Eva was resting soundly in her seat.

"She's so precious," whispered Grace.

Liz looked tenderly at Eva. Though she didn't say a word, Gina knew her friend loved her goddaughter fiercely. Gina sent up a silent prayer that Liz would find a man to bring her abundant love and that God would bless them with beautiful children, as He had blessed Gina.

"You love your sister so much, don't you, AJ?"

whispered Liz as she knelt down to his level.

"I love my sissy soooooo much."

When everyone in the room laughed, AJ raised his finger to his lips, signaling not to wake his sister. They moved back to the kitchen, where Liz and Grace helped themselves to the freshly-baked sugar cookies on the counter. AJ plopped himself in the chair between Grace and Elizabeth and helped himself to some chips, and Gina reveled in his happiness.

"Look who's awake," said Christian, entering the room, with Eva in his arms. Elizabeth immediately shoved down her last bite and stood up to steal her goddaughter from her father.

"Let me hold that precious girl of yours."

"Fine, but I'm next," said Grace. "Don't be dilly-dallying."

Elizabeth rolled her eyes at Gina in jest. "Who says dilly-dallying anymore?"

"Either you are making fun of my age or my Southern roots, but I don't care. In ten minutes, I'm taking that baby from you, so get your fill now."

Gina joked with her friends and family for the next half hour, and it was almost perfect. It would have been if she wasn't so worried about Anna.

"Alright, kiddos, let's let these women have their girls' night," said Christian.

"I want to stay, Dad!"

"You can't."

"Why?"

"Because we have to put Eva to bed and start our boys' night."

The grin that took over his face was enough to light the room. "Night, Miss Grace, Night, Miss Liz. I'm going to boys' night with my dad!"

"What are you going to do?" asked Liz.

"I don't know, but I'll be with my dad, so it's gonna be awesome."

The collective awwws erupted at once, then Christian walked over and planted a tender kiss on Gina's cheek, said his goodbyes, and left the women alone.

"I'm practically swooning, you know," said Elizabeth.

"You? I'm about to go find myself a man after that beautiful exchange," joked Grace.

"Speaking of men. Are you still talking to your ex?"

"Real smooth."

"Well, as long as she mentioned it," said Gina, leaning in.

"We've been talking, yes, and it's nice. I don't want to rush it or make any presumptions. So, for now, I'm just enjoying having him back in my life—in a positive way. We seem to be letting go of the bitterness and the hurt and getting to know each other again."

"I'm so happy for you," said Gina.

"Well, it's nothing like the picture-perfect family going on over here, but you know we all can't have what you do."

Gina noticed the second Grace realized what she said when a horrified look appeared on her face.

"Stop! I don't want to hear an apology out of you, got it?"

"How did you--?"

"Because I know you, Grace."

"But, Gina, I can't believe I said that. I just meant that it's so nice to see you happy, especially since when we met, you were anything but."

"I know, Grace, but look at my life now."

"You're glowing, Gina," said Elizabeth. "I love seeing you this way. I know it doesn't take away the past ..."

"It doesn't, but it shows the power of God's healing and His perfect plan for all of us. So, let's talk about Anna."

Suddenly her two friends were silent for the first time that night.

"There's nothing to report on our end," said Elizabeth. "Both Grace and I have called and texted her, and besides a terse, 'I'm fine,' she's not sharing anything with us."

"She's right, Gina," said Elizabeth. "You're the only one she opens up to. Are you okay with that?"

"What do you mean? Of course, I'm okay with that. She's my sister."

Grace and Elizabeth exchanged glances.

"Oh, you mean because Anna is all depressed, and you think she is going to make me fall back into despair? I'm fine, girls. It actually makes me happy that she is comfortable talking to me."

"So, you're not getting depressed again?"

"No, Liz, I'm not. I know everyone was worried about me there for a while after I had Eva. And yeah, I know I was acting crazy and jealous, but that's what hormones do to you. And yes, I have a history of depression after everything I've been through, and I have to keep an eye on it, but I'm good."

The relief in their eyes was evident to Gina, and she thanked God for blessing her with such loyal friends.

"Listen, I know we are worried about Anna, but I

have to tell you I'm concerned about Tony, too," said Elizabeth.

"So am I," said Gina, "especially after everything that happened in the past week."

"What are you talking about?" asked Grace.

Gina filled them in on the chaos of Garrett and his machinations against Tony and Anna. Elizabeth put her head in her hands and fell silent. Gina knew those two had become close in the past few years, and her heart ached for Liz.

"Well, if I wasn't freaking out before, now it's ten times worse. And I'm furious. Tony and Anna were on their way to being so happy, and that jerk messed it up, and no one is doing anything to fix it! Not even the church!"

"I know, Liz, but you can't go in there guns blazing and make things worse. We just need to be there for our friends."

"Has Christian talked to Tony?"

"He tried, but now I realize he has to do more. We are all so focused on Anna that I don't think we realized how much this affects Tony."

She planned on talking to her husband about that later that night.

~

The knock sounded, and Tony prayed that whoever was there would go away. He knew it wasn't Anna, and she was the only person he wanted to see.

"Tony. I know you're in there. I can hear the TV. I'm not leaving."

Tony turned off the TV, not that he was watching it anyway, and opened the door for Christian.

"Hey, man, you're not looking so hot."

"Is that your way of cheering me up?"

"No, I came to tell you that I'm here for you. And it may not seem like it now, but it will get better."

Tony looked at his friend and suddenly felt like a jerk. Here he was depressed over Anna when Christian had endured so much more when he lost his brother and niece. Not to mention all the struggles he and Gina went through before they made their way back to each other.

"I love your sister, you know."

"I do. And I couldn't be happier about that. And Anna feels the same way, you just need to let her deal with this in her own way, and when she comes through it, you will be there."

"You're her brother. How do you not want to beat the crap out of Garrett for everything he put her through?"

"Bro, I have to fight that sensation every day. But doing that won't help my sister, and she is who I am worried about—and you."

"Have you seen her lately?"

"No, she's ignoring all of us, if that makes you feel better."

"It doesn't. Because she doesn't hate you guys."

"She doesn't hate you either. She is hurt, and like I said, you have to give her time."

"She is all alone, Chris, aren't you worried?"

"Of course, I am, but the only good thing about this is she isn't. The one person she will talk to is my wife—and I thank God for that small blessing. Speaking of which, are you still talking to God?"

"You know my faith is everything to me. It is the only thing that is getting me through this. Even before all this happened, I prayed God would bring us together, and He did."

"Then you have to keep that faith."

Tony wondered if Christian was worried that Gina was the sole person bearing the brunt of Anna's pain. He had to be concerned about that effect on her. But he still felt odd bringing that up, considering he dated Gina for a brief period when Christian and Gina were still figuring things out.

"What else is bothering you?"

Tony was grateful he had such a perceptive friend who was there for him.

"I'm wondering if your wife is okay taking the job as Anna's therapist, but I'm afraid to ask you that."

"Still carrying the torch for my wife, I see," he said while giving him a friendly jab in the arm. "I'm kidding. I'm glad you two are friends, especially since I have hope you will be part of the family someday."

Tony looked down at his hands, avoiding his friend's discerning gaze. He once dreamt about that too and had faith it would happen. But now, all Tony felt was doubt. He took the easy way out and changed the subject.

"Speaking of family, how's your mom doing with all this? She must be losing it."

"She is worried about her, yes. But surprisingly, my dad is the one really taking this hard."

It made sense that John was angry after what Garrett did to his daughter. He was a cop, so he knew the bad things that happened every day. It must be killing him.

"You will be shocked to hear this, but my mom is actually giving her space."

"Wow, has hell frozen over?" he said with a laugh.

"It's good to hear you laugh, man. You will get through this. You both will."

"Thanks, Chris."

~

Anna lie on the couch, scrolling through the photos of her and Tony. She shouldn't be torturing herself but couldn't help it. She was still furious with him, but the ache in her heart was worse. She yearned for their daily talks and texts. She felt empty now. And the anger—Anna never experienced emotions like this even after Alex and Teresa died. That was a terrible accident, but what Garrett did to her was inexcusable. Even worse was Pastor Tom ignoring it. But the anger toward Tony was starting to fade. Anna knew his actions were because he cared about her. Still, she wasn't ready to forgive.

She heard the ding, then saw the text pop up from her mom. "I canceled family dinner today. But Gina and I are bringing it to you." She smiled at her mom's message, which was thoughtful, and quite the improvement for her. In the past, she would have ordered Anna to her house with an ultimatum. Her mom never canceled Sunday dinner except maybe right after Alex and Teresa died. Her mother was softening, and she knew everything the family went through after that tragedy, then finally welcoming Gina back was the reason for that. Once again, Gina was the person helping them heal. The guilt consumed her that they weren't there for Gina when she needed them most.

"What's for dinner?" was all she texted back.

"All your favorites," was the response, and Anna was slightly looking forward to it.

~

As soon as Anna opened the door, Helena enveloped her daughter in her arms, surprising Anna for the second time that day. She expected her mother to come barreling in with trays of food and barking orders. It was so out of the ordinary that tears sprang to her eyes.

"Anna, what's wrong? I didn't mean to make you cry. We are supposed to be cheering you up, not the opposite."

"I'm fine, Mom. You just caught me off guard, that's all."

"By hugging you? I'm sorry, am I that bad?"

"You're not bad at all, I just know you comfort through food, so I expected you to come in here and start feeding me."

"Well, I plan on doing that, don't you worry. In fact, why don't you two help me bring the food inside? It's still hot, so we can enjoy it all now."

"Sounds great, Mom, thank you."

Anna was surprised at how much she enjoyed the meal with her mom and Gina. They laughed and talked like a bunch of girlfriends, and she wasn't sure the three of them had ever done that before.

"No offense, but I think we need to ditch the kids and men more often," joked Anna. "I really enjoyed this. Thank you both."

"You're welcome, Anna. But you know I'm not leaving here and letting you go back to your binge-watching TV and escaping reality."

"Mom."

"Let me finish. I see those articles in the paper your boss has been assigning, and it's beneath you. There is only so much time he is going to give you before he tells you to jump back in."

"He already has. I return to my regular news beat tomorrow."

"Are you ready?"

"I know it's the right thing. I have to stop feeling sorry for myself. I just can't figure out how."

Gina patted her hand. "You will, Anna. Just keep trusting in God and reach out to your friends and family."

"I know. Having both of you here today made me realize that. I'm sorry I pushed you away, Mom."

"It's okay. I'm glad you had Gina to help you through it."

The old Helena would have said that as a jab, but Anna knew that's not how she meant it now. At least she didn't think it was. Sometimes it was hard to tell with her mother.

"Mom, you're not upset I didn't turn to you, right?"

Gina interrupted. "I could never take your place, Helena."

"Girls, stop. I'm so sorry that I acted in a way in the past that makes you think I'm upset with you. The exact opposite is true. Gina, I apologize for how I treated you after the accident—that I turned everyone against you."

"Helena—"

"Let me finish. I will regret that behavior until the day I die. I know you have forgiven me long ago, but seeing Anna depressed these past few weeks makes me realize how bad it was when you were all alone with your grief. Yet here you are comforting Anna when you could have just turned away."

Anna saw the tears streaming down Gina's cheeks.

"You are a remarkable woman, and I don't tell you that enough. I would like to thank you for loving my son, for loving my daughter, and for being there for this family, even when things are tough for you."

"Thank you, Helena. I love you."

"I love you too.

"But listen to me, both of you," said Gina firmly. "We are done apologizing. That was a rough time for all of us, as we were knee-deep in grief. Just look at where this family is now and what God has brought us through. Deal? No more talk of the past?"

"Deal," said Helena and Anna at the same time, which made them all laugh.

Anna knew the conversation would turn to her, but suddenly, she wasn't dreading it. She leaned back on the couch, took a deep breath, and waited for her mother's questions. The one that came first was not at all what she expected.

"Have you called the pastor yet?"

"No, Mom."

"Your father and I didn't raise a quitter, Anna."

Wow, way to get right to it. Anna figured her questions would be about Tony and how she needed to forgive him so she could get married and have a family. That used to be her mother's focus.

"She's right, Anna. I know it's not easy, but you have to tell the truth."

"You two realize that what you are telling me to do is the exact reason I'm not talking to Tony. Do you want me to shut you out too?"

"You're not talking to Tony because he did what you were too terrified to do," said Helena.

"I'm not afraid. This is my battle, and no one has

the right to tell me how to fight it."

"But that's the thing, Anna, you aren't fighting at all. You gave up without even trying."

"It wouldn't make a difference. The pastor doesn't believe Tony, so why would he believe me?

"You have to try," said Gina. "It's different coming from the source."

"But Tony has known Pastor Tom longer than me. He should believe him. If he doesn't, there is no way he will trust me.

"Still, you won't know because you never tried," said Helena.

"And you're giving Garrett power over you. You're letting him win," said Gina.

"How am I letting him win? I'm depressed, and I let go of the only guy I ever loved before we even got started."

"You made all those choices, Anna," said her mother.

Were they right? Was everything that happened of her own doing? Was she blaming everyone else instead of herself?

Her guests seemed to realize they got to her as they quietly got up, kissed her on the cheek before saying goodbye, and left her to evaluate her screwed-up choices.

Chapter 19

A week passed since the conversation with her mother and Gina, and their words never left her. The only time it wasn't in her head was when she daydreamed of Tony. The scenes that played in a loop were those moments on the baseball field when they discovered they were more than friends. When she spotted him looking for her in the stands, when their eyes connected, and she witnessed his excitement at seeing her there. The few words they shared after the games. The caring he showed to his players. Tony was an amazing man, and she missed every little thing about him.

Her boss walked over to her desk, jolting her back to reality.

"I have a big assignment for you, Anna. Meet me in my office in five minutes."

She walked out of Dan's office with a pile of info from news clippings to police reports. She had a mountain of work to do but was looking forward to it, even though this would be a challenging story. A sophomore at the local university said she was raped, but the school allegedly covered it up. As stories go, it has been played out at college campuses throughout the country over the years, but it's never happened here. She was grateful Dan trusted her with the assignment.

Anna knew she was their best reporter, but still, her head wasn't exactly in the game lately. Maybe this was the distraction she needed.

Several hours later, Dan was headed out for the night, and it was evident to Anna he was surprised to see her still there.

"Anna, I didn't mean you had to write the whole thing tonight," he joked.

"I know. But once I get started in my research, it's hard to pull back."

"That's one of the things that makes you such a great reporter—your quest for the truth—the real story. But you've been at it enough tonight. Come on, let's walk out together."

Anna couldn't move. She imagined the color drained from her face from the way Dan was eyeing her.

"Anna, what's wrong?"

She willed her tears to stay in her eyelids. She refused to cry in front of her boss.

"Nothing, I'm good. Let's go."

She walked out with him in silence, uttered a quick goodbye, then jumped in her car and let the tears flow and the prayers pour out.

"Dear Lord, help me. Why do I see the truth in my job but am rendered immobile when it's time for me to face the truth? Please help me, Lord. Tell me what to do."

Then she picked up her phone and texted.

"Hey."

"Hey, is everything okay?"

"Not really. Will you pray for me?"

"I pray for you every day."

"Why?"

"Because I love you, and I care about you."

"Even after everything?"

"Yes, Anna. I told you we aren't over. We will get through this, and when you are ready to come back to me, I will be here."

"Anna? Are you still there? I'm calling you."

"No!"

She knew that was harsh, but she would fall apart if she heard his voice on the phone. She wasn't ready to go back to him. She had to figure this out for herself first. When he didn't reply, she knew she hurt him.

"Tony, I'm sorry. I'm just not ready. If I talk to you, it would be so easy ... I can't—not yet."

"Yet? You just gave me hope, Anna."

"Night, Tony."

"Night, Anna."

~

Tony knew they had a lot to work out, but the exchange with Anna gave him optimism. Still, he had so much nervous energy to shed. He usually looked forward to summer break, but this year he counted the days until they were back in school and his work could occupy the space in his mind. His original plan for the summer was to volunteer at the church, but that was out. He couldn't bear running into Pastor Tom or Garrett, or even Erica. So that's why it was Sunday, and he was sitting in the pews at a new church.

~

"Open the door, Anna."

The door swung open, and Anna took in Elizabeth, dressed in a cute pale yellow sundress that she had never seen before.

197

"Do you like it?" she asked while entering her apartment without an invitation. "I had to choose it myself since my shopping buddy is ghosting me."

"I see you haven't lost your touch for the dramatic. And why are you here so early on a Sunday morning?"

"Because Sunday mornings we go to church, and we have stayed away long enough."

"Are you crazy? Clearly, you don't know me at all if you think I'm stepping foot in that place after everything that happened."

"Sorry, I should have clarified. We aren't going to First United. Last week, I tried the Methodist Church downtown and really liked it. It's pretty similar, and I think you will enjoy it."

She knew fighting with Liz was futile, so she told her she would be ready in about ten minutes and went to her room. She missed her Sunday morning traditions. Maybe this would be good for her.

"I'm ready. And Liz, thanks for doing this. You're a good friend."

"I know, let's go."

"And so modest too."

They pulled into the parking lot, and Liz and Anna saw it at the same time—Tony's truck.

"I can't believe you!" Anna yelled to her friend.

"Anna, I promise you, I had no idea he would be here. I haven't even talked to him. He's been shutting me out, just like you have."

That hurt. Anna knew it was true, but Liz was close with Tony too, so she felt guilty for the role she may have played in those two not talking either. She took a deep breath, looked at her friend, gave her a nod, and opened the door.

Anna entered the church, practically attached to Liz, and searched for Tony. When she spotted him on the far side of the sanctuary, she nudged Liz and pointed to the seats right in front of them, which happened to offer a quick escape if needed.

Anna enjoyed the service, and for parts of it, she didn't turn her head to look at Tony. But it was almost impossible. She noticed the stubble on his face, signifying he didn't shave that morning. He wore a dark blue polo that fit him just right, but the most appealing thing about him was his countenance. He sang with the band during worship time, and he seemed to take in every word of the sermon, which was focused on perseverance. As soon as the pastor prayed the final blessing, Anna stole one glance, then grabbed her friend's hand and led her to the car.

~

Tony was pleasantly surprised at how much he enjoyed the service and could picture himself sitting in those pews every week and forming new relationships. He knew Elizabeth and Anna would be at home there, too, so he sent off a group text from the church parking lot.

"Hey, I just wanted to let you both know I tried the Methodist church downtown and really liked it. You two should check it out."

He looked down to see Elizabeth reply immediately. "We went today and loved it!"

"You were there?"

"Yes. We sat by the door and left as soon as church was over."

They were there. Tony wondered if they spotted him, and he hoped they didn't. Because if the answer was yes, and his two friends ignored him, then the hole in his heart just split wide open.

~

Anna was hunched over her desk all day throwing herself into the article but ignored the next step—talking to the victim. It was a big deal that the student agreed to be interviewed, and Dan was ecstatic about it. Still, for the first time in her career, Anna dreaded an interview. She looked over her questions yet again, though she could recite them by heart. Then she bowed her head and prayed that God would get her through what she suspected may be the most challenging interview of her life.

Anna sat at the round kitchen table across from Stella, a beautiful girl with a golden tan and brown hair that reached her shoulders. Anna admired her big brown eyes but wished she could steal more than a few glimpses. The girl was withdrawn and only looked up at Anna once since she arrived ten minutes ago. Stella was a younger version of her mother Audrey, a woman just as beautiful. Anna observed that same sadness in her eyes but also a fierce determination. It was time to get started, so Anna sent up another silent prayer that God would bring her through this unscathed.

"Stella, I read all the documents associated with what happened to you. But I hope you can tell me in your own words."

Audrey squeezed her daughter's hand tighter and nodded, giving her approval to share her story.

Stella went over the events of that night, and sadly it was a tale that plays out across college campuses across the country. Girl meets boy, girl acts interested, boy goes too far, girl says stop, boy doesn't listen, and the fate of that girl is forever changed.

Anna listened to Stella and wondered what she was like before the incident. She pictured her laughing with friends, her head thrown back, an easygoing air about her. If Anna was right, she hoped that carefree existence wasn't lost forever. Anna pressed on and thanked God for helping her through this interview.

"Thank you for sharing those details with me, Stella. I know it was difficult, and I must ask some hard questions."

She nodded, giving Anna permission to continue.

"I know you are pressing charges. Why is it important for you to do that?"

"Because he can't do this to another girl." She said it with a voice of authority and revealed another version of herself. Anna looked up from her notes in surprise and pressed on.

"Was that a difficult decision for you?"

"No."

Just like that. No pause, nothing, just pure confidence in her words.

"Was there any part of you that wanted to move on and put this behind you?"

"Of course. But God keeps telling me, again and again, this is what I need to do. So as hard as this is, I know He will get me through it."

Anna looked at her pen as she wrote and could see it wavering from left to right as her hands started to tremble. She knew the two women across from her noticed it too, but she vowed to finish this meeting with her emotions intact.

Before Anna could recall her next question, Stella continued.

"I know people don't understand why I want to press charges, but if I don't, he will harm other girls. Women need to speak up more. Even if it's not rape, like it was for me, men can't think they can overpower and control us. We must tell the truth when men bully and hurt us, even if the situation isn't as extreme as mine. That's what I learned from this situation."

Anna put down her pen, as she was tired of seeing it tremble in her hands.

"Are you okay?" asked Audrey. "Can I get you some more water?"

"Yes, please," she managed to get out.

"Did you go through something like me?" asked Stella, as soon as her mother left the room.

"It wasn't even close to what happened to you." Did Anna just answer her that fast?

Stella reached her hand across the table. "But it still hurts."

"It does."

Audrey quietly re-entered, set the water in front of Anna, shared a glance with her daughter, and exited silently.

"Want to talk about it?"

"Maybe another time. But I admire your strength. And I thank you for meeting with me to tell your story. I have a feeling you will touch the hearts of many and will encourage other women out there to speak out."

"What about you, Anna? Are you going to let whoever hurt you get away with it and do damage to others?"

Her stomach twisted at the question that may as well play on repeat now.

"I'm sorry."

"Don't be. And the answer is I don't know."

~

Anna couldn't shake her conversation with Stella. At first, she seemed similar to her, in that you could see the sadness in her eyes. But when she asked her about confronting her attacker, she turned into this fierce woman who was simply standing up for what was right. It was no different from what everyone else had been telling Anna. When Stella said it, what Garrett did to her hit home. She refused to stay silent any longer. Without allowing herself time to chicken out, she dialed Pastor Tom's number, and he answered on the second ring.

"Anna, it's so nice to hear from you. How are you?" The caller ID must have warned him, and she figured it was a good sign that he took her call, but his response floored her. How was she? How was she supposed to answer that? But then again, he gave no credence to what Tony told him, so maybe he thought everything was normal.

"I'm not good, Pastor. Everything Tony relayed was true. I now have the courage to tell you myself, and I want you to investigate the matter."

The silence reverberated through the phone.

"Pastor Tom?"

"I'm here. These are some heavy accusations, Anna."

"It's the truth. Why are you turning a blind eye without asking a single question?"

"Garrett is on the worship team."

Her blood pressure shot sky-high. She collected her breath and wished Tony was by her side for this call.

"So that means he's a better Christian than I am? I

don't even know what you mean by that. It's ludicrous."

"Calm down, Anna. I just mean that I have to tread lightly."

"Why?" She was getting hysterical now, and any amount of yoga breathing or trying to calm down was pointless. If Tony were here, he would stroke her hand and make her feel like she wasn't alone.

"I told you. He is a staff member."

"Even more of a reason you need to investigate this."

"Give me some time, and I will get back to you."

She hung up the phone and tried to gain her equilibrium. This is where speaking out landed her. Dismissed without an ounce of guilt or concern for her well-being. She would have called someone if words could come out of her mouth, but the sobs were coming too violently.

She sent off a group text to Gina and her mom. "Please come over."

~

Anna was slightly calmer now. She sat on the couch, a hot cup of tea in her hand, with her mom seated on one side and Gina on the other. Gina explained that just because we have God in our life doesn't make things easier for us. Still, He is there always, and we have to keep relying on Him. On the other hand, her mother was seething but doing an impressive job of hiding most of it. But Anna had witnessed her mother's anger. She deserved an Oscar for how well she was hiding her feelings regarding Garrett. Anna was certain Pastor Tom would get a call from her mother, and she no longer cared. Anna was flaming mad herself, and now she possessed that feistiness she admired in Stella earlier today. Anna thanked God for bringing Stella into her life. It was just what she needed. She knew she had to apologize to Tony and would do that as soon as Gina and her mom left, and now that she wasn't a blubbering mess.

"Are you going to call Tony?" her mother asked.

Anna smiled. "Wow, mother's intuition must be a real thing. Yes, I will call him later."

"Good girl, Anna. That boy loves you, and his heart is in the right place."

"I know, Mom. Thanks!"

~

Tony saw her name on his phone and wished he had the resolve not to get it, but he was all in when it came to Anna. He was still hurt that she was shutting him out, but that didn't matter.

"Hey, Anna."

"Hey, Tony. Do you have a minute?"

"Sure."

He felt a sadness that this was what their relationship had become.

"I'm sorry."

He wanted to hear it, but now that he did, there were no words of gratitude that would come out.

"For?"

"For everything. You were right. I had to realize that myself and I did today. I hope one day I can tell you the details, but for now, I just wanted you to know I'm so sorry."

"I forgive you, Anna. I feel like there's more."

"There is. I called Pastor Tom today."

"That's great, Anna. I know that took courage, and I

205

am so proud of you."

"Thanks, but he didn't listen to me either."

"What?" he yelled through the phone.

"Did you really think he would?"

"Of course I did. That's why I told you to say something. I wouldn't have set you up for disappointment. I can't believe he won't even look into it."

"Calm down, Tony."

"How can I when this is happening to you? You clearly have no idea how much you mean to me."

And then he was gone.

Chapter 20

In the weeks since the article on Stella was published, Anna existed in a world full of chaos and contentment. Her reporting forced the college to look into the matter. Stella's attacker was no longer a student there, and charges against him were pending. And she gained a new friend. Though Stella was much younger than Anna, they had become close through the interview process and now talked regularly. Stella didn't push, but she dropped regular hints to Anna about how important it is to tell the truth and ensure people are responsible for their actions. She was about to leave work and meet her for coffee when Dan walked up.

"Hey, Anna, did you see the latest round of letters?"

"I did. I keep waiting for the amount to get smaller, but it never happens."

Since Anna's article, women have sent letters and emails to share their stories and thank Anna for reporting on Stella's case.

"You did good, kid."

Anna playfully rolled her eyes at her middle-aged boss. She bristled each time he called her kid, but he was about the age of her own father. He meant it endearingly, so she let it roll.

"Are you okay? I've been worried about you lately.

You seem off."

"I have some stuff going on, but it's fine. Throwing myself into the reporting helped, so thanks for that."

"You got it, Ace."

She rolled her eyes again. Dan laughed and walked away while she headed out to meet Stella.

~

Anna sipped her coffee and listened as Stella relayed yet another story that made her laugh. She was so thankful this girl came into her life at a time when she needed it. Suddenly, though, her friend paused, and it seemed like she was intent on observing something take place behind Anna.

"What's so interesting?"

"Sorry, don't turn around. I didn't realize I was staring. I'm being judgy, but there is this guy back there that just seems slimy, if you know what I mean."

"Slimy? Well, gee, you are killing me. Now I have to look."

"Don't! He is moving toward the counter. You will see him eventually."

"Got it. Are you sure that you aren't still reeling from everything that has happened and that every guy is slimy?"

"No, wait until you spot this guy. My spidey senses are tingling."

Anna laughed, kept drinking her coffee, then almost choked on it when she identified the subject of Stella's comments.

Garrett saw her and immediately kept walking, but Erica stopped at their table. "Anna, how are you? I was telling Tony recently how much we miss you guys at church. Why did you

208

leave?"

Anna had no idea where the courage came from, but the words spilled out freely.

"I don't want to talk about it. But Garrett has an idea. So does Pastor Tom. You should ask them."

Garrett grimaced for a split second. He recovered quickly, but she swore Erica noted his disdain. The awkwardness at the table was thick, so she wasn't surprised when Erica uttered an uncomfortable goodbye and walked away.

"That's it. Let's go," said Stella, grabbing Anna's hand and leading her out of the coffee shop. "We're going for a walk, and you are going to tell me all about slime ball and why that encounter has you shaking like a leaf."

An hour later, the two women were seated at a bench facing the water, and Stella was still processing everything Anna told her about Garrett.

"I knew this would happen. This is why I didn't want to tell you about Garrett."

"Wait, what do you mean?" said Stella, looking at her with confusion.

"I knew you would judge me for not speaking up."

"That's not what I'm doing, Anna. And you did speak up."

"Yeah, but only after I met you."

"Well, then God brought us together to help each other. I'm incredibly proud of you."

"For what?"

"Let's see. For not tackling Garrett to the ground in the coffee shop. For not screaming at Pastor Tom for ignoring your story. Shall I go on?"

Anna just stared at her new friend. Ever since all of

this happened, the only feelings she had were of failure. But here was Stella applauding her for exhibiting self-control.

Stella went on. "I can't believe that girl is still with him. What did she say when you told her what he did to you?"

Anna knew the color had drained out of her face, and she could only imagine the look of shame that resided there.

"Anna! Please tell me you told her what happened?"

"Why, Stella? Garrett will just call me a liar. No one believes me. Why would she be any different?"

Stella didn't utter a word, and in the silence, all Anna could think of was how she disappointed yet another person in her life.

~

Tony sat in the pew closest to the entrance. If Elizabeth and Anna showed up, they wouldn't be able to ignore him this time. He picked up his phone to call Anna at least a dozen times in the past week but never went through with it. Tony wanted to tell her she did a great job telling Stella's story but knew it would bring up everything she endured and didn't want to cause her more pain. So, he was acting like his high school students—plotting a plan to run into her, so he could catch a glimpse of the person who lit him up whenever she entered a room.

He saw Elizabeth first and caught her eye, willing her to come over and sit by him. He knew Elizabeth was rooting for their relationship, so he prayed she would help him with his sophomoric efforts. When she turned toward the back of the church with Anna following behind, she sent him a look of apology.

Ultimately, her loyalty was with Anna, so Tony sat through the service alone. He doubted Anna even cared he was there.

~

Anna spotted Tony as soon as they walked in. The urge to slide in right next to him and hold his hand overpowered her. She wanted him to know how much she missed him, how her thoughts turned to him every day. But she couldn't act like nothing was wrong. She knew now that he went to the pastor because he cared, but she was all messed up over Garrett and couldn't deal with her feelings for Tony right now. So, when Elizabeth spotted him and steered her the other way, she was both relieved and shattered all at once.

~

Anna drooled at the fresh omelet in front of her and had to admit she felt a little more like herself. She was glad Elizabeth forced her to come to breakfast with her.

"What are you gloating about?" she asked her friend.

"Admit it."

"Fine, you were right. Go ahead and rub it in my face."

"I will do no such thing. But I will remind you of this very moment the next time you try to run back to your apartment and hide."

"Well, then what are you doing later? Because I'm dreading dinner at my mother's."

"You know you have to go. I'm shocked Helena let you stay away this long. That's huge for her."

"I get that she's worried about me. So that's why I'm going. And I do miss them."

Elizabeth's face changed before her, and Anna

211

suddenly felt the anxiousness seep back into her veins. What was wrong now?

"Don't look now, but Erica is on her way over here, and she doesn't look happy."

Before Anna could process what was happening, Erica pulled up a chair next to her. Her typically slick hair was disheveled, and she looked like she didn't add any makeup to her always flawlessly made-up face.

"You have to tell me what happened between you and Garrett."

Anna exchanged glances with Elizabeth, and Erica pounced.

"See. I saw how you two looked at each other. I need to know."

"Why?" They both said at once.

"Because I'm getting a weird feeling."

"Listen, Erica. We like you. But besides hanging out at church, we don't know a ton about you. What happened between those two is personal," Elizabeth said while gesturing to Anna.

Erica's harsh demeanor seemed to soften a bit, and instead of coming in guns blazing, she took another tactic.

"I'm not getting a good vibe around him."

"You're going to have to give us more than that. I'm not going to pour my heart out to you. Garrett is not a good guy, and I have no idea if he sent you over here to encourage me to confide in you," said Anna.

"Why isn't he a good guy?"

Anna was frustrated now.

"I don't know, Erica. You tell us!"

"Fine, if you don't want to talk, I will figure it out on my own."

She left the table and immediately picked up her phone and started typing.

"You think she's texting him?" asked Elizabeth.

"I would almost bet on it. I don't know Erica that well, but that definitely isn't behavior she has shown in the past."

"And we all know how manipulative he can be," Elizabeth finished.

"That's exactly what has me worried."

"What are you going to do?"

"Right now, I'm going home, grabbing my stuff, and going out on the water. That always makes me feel better."

"I'm proud of you, Anna."

"For what?"

"Even a week ago, you would have run home and huddled under the covers to hide. I know things are still tough for you, but I'm noticing a difference. I think writing that story and meeting Stella was good for you."

Anna didn't know what to say, but she knew her friend was right. She was still broken inside, and her heart ached for Tony every second, but maybe things would turn around if she started living and stopped cowering in fear.

Chapter 21

Go to her.

Tony heard God's voice repeatedly since he left the church a few hours ago. His heart pounded in his chest, fearful that she would turn him away, but God had gotten him this far in life. He wasn't about to question Him now. He pulled up to Anna's just as she was packing gear in her car. He took a breath and jumped out to greet her.

"Tony," was all she said.

"I couldn't stay away, Anna. You may not believe me, but God was calling me here to you ever since I left church today. I was going to ask if you wanted to go out on the water. I have all my stuff, and it looks like that's where you are headed too."

"I'll meet you there."

He knew he looked stunned but sent up a silent prayer of thanks to God and drove to the water, thinking he would follow her anywhere. When he arrived, she leaned against her car, with the sun on her face. He was captivated, as always, by her beauty. He hopped out of his truck, and she stopped him with a gentle touch on his arm before he could pull out his board. The electricity shot through him, and he wondered if he could do this. Be this close to her, yet so distant. Her voice interrupted him.

"Can we not talk about everything going on and just enjoy the day?"

He nodded and followed her to the water's edge. An hour later, they stopped paddling and floated on their boards, enjoying the slight coolness of the water. After all, the temperature was still in the nineties, and the Gulf temperature was warm. They hadn't said much to each other, staying on safe subjects, which meant almost nothing about Anna and everything about Tony. He told her he looked forward to the school year starting again and how he had been helping his dad with projects around the house. They talked about Christian and Gina and how Eva was getting bigger each day, smiling and giggling and wrapping everyone around her cute little finger.

He laid on his board, not wanting to return to reality but knowing they would have to soon. He stole a glance at Anna, resting peacefully, and he prayed this was the beginning of their way back to each other. A few moments later, the spunky voice he missed so much was egging him on.

"What do you say, coach? Race ya back?"

"Get ready to eat my dust." Then they paddled back to the dock in record time, both exhausted and exhilarated. Anna only finished a few strokes behind him.

"Way to go, coach. When did you get so good at this?"

"I've been out here a lot."

She looked at him quizzically.

"It makes me feel close to you."

He saw her exhale, and he wouldn't say anything further, but he was always honest with Anna.

"Well, thanks for today. It was nice."

"You're welcome."

Then he walked to his car, packed up his board, and drove away, leaving her there looking after him. It took all his restraint to not push, not ask her to spend more time with him, to tell her he missed her so much it hurt. Then he wondered if she was affected by today at all.

~

Anna showed up at her mother's early, anxious to download what happened with Tony. She was thrilled to see her brother's car and headed into the house that was full of laughter and chaos.

"Aunt Anna's here!" yelled AJ, as he plowed into her and wrapped his little arms around her slim legs.

"Aunt Anna's here," her dad echoed and pulled her into his strong arms. "You not only showed up but got here early. You made my day, honey."

"I'm glad, but you know I really came early to talk to Mom and Gina. So, go on, you boys scoot," she teased.

Gina and her mother exchanged a smile while her mother stopped cooking and took a seat at the table.

"Spill it," they both said in unison.

"Do you want the good or bad first?"

"When is the bad going to stop?" uttered her mother.

"Sorry, Mom."

"No, I'm sorry. I shouldn't have said that. I've just been so worried about you. Give us the bad, so we end on a high note."

"Excellent idea," Gina agreed.

Once she relayed the story about Erica, Anna paused and was anxious to hear what they thought about it all.

"I don't know what to think," said Gina.

"I agree. On the one hand, I kind of feel sorry for Erica, but on the other, I don't have a good feeling about it. Garrett is manipulating her somehow."

Anna agreed with her mother, then figured she would move forward to the good part. Her mother and Gina leaned forward, listening intently with eagerness written on their faces, their mouths upturned, and it made her heart happy.

"Oh, Anna. I knew you two would find your way back to each other."

"Mom!"

"I know, I know. You have a long way to go, but it's an important first step. You have been through so much, and I am so incredibly proud of your strength through all this. I'm in awe of you."

"Me too," said Gina, reaching over and giving her hand a soft squeeze.

Anna grabbed a stray napkin from the table and wiped away a few tears. "Yeesh, I thought I could go a day without crying." They all laughed, and for the first time in a long while, Anna thought maybe she would be okay.

~

It had been almost a week since Tony spent time with Anna, and he was hopeful it was the beginning of their journey back to each other. They exchanged some texts and even a quick call or two, and at times, it was almost as if nothing had changed. The distance still existed, but there were moments where he glimpsed the old Anna—full of life and love before Garrett quenched some of her spirit.

He was thrilled to be spending time with Christian again too. He sat at Nick's, the local bar they all enjoyed, and waited for his friend to arrive.

"Hey, man, sorry I'm late. I wanted to help Gina get the kids ready for bed before I headed out."

"No worries. I'm glad we could meet. It's been a long time."

"I know. It's hard to get away sometimes with the little ones."

Christian's voice trailed off, and Tony hated the awkwardness that lingered now that he and Anna were ... whatever they were. Before Tony could second-guess whether or not to bring her up, Christian decided for him.

"So, I heard you are talking to my sister again."

"Yeah, what did she tell you?" He felt the smile on his cheeks and tried to tamp it down. He knew Christian would give him a good ribbing for that one.

"Nothing. It's my mom and Gina who gave me some hints. I'm actually surprised to see you in such a good mood. I figured you would be planning Garrett's demise by now after what happened. I can't believe he is pulling Erica into all this now. I hope that girl is careful."

Tony put down his beer and took a deep breath. He tried to hide what was going on in his head, but it was too late. Christian realized Tony had no clue what he was talking about. Once again, Anna retreated from Tony when he was dumb enough to think they were headed back toward each other. Christian put his head in his hands, and Tony saw the struggle taking place as he realized the information he divulged.

"I'm so sorry. I'm sure Anna didn't want to worry

you. She was probably so excited to be talking to you again that messing all that up was the last thing on her mind."

"It's fine."

Christian kept talking in an attempt to ease the tension. "It's not like she told me either—I found out from my mom and Gina. She doesn't want us going all caveman and protecting her. You know how strong my sister is, and she wants to take care of everything herself."

"Really, man, it's okay. Maybe I was naïve to think we were growing close again. And as much as I'm dying to ask you what that jerk did this time, I'm not." Tony took the last swig of his beer and told Christian he was calling it a night.

~

"Hey, Christian, what's up?"

"I messed up bad, Anna."

"What do you mean?"

"I met Tony tonight and mentioned that something else had happened with Garrett."

"Christian!"

"I'm sorry. He was so happy you guys were talking again that I figured he knew."

"Why would I tell him that? Part of the reason it was so good between us is that we didn't discuss all that stuff. What did he say when you told him what happened?"

"That's the thing. I only alluded to it. When I went to offer details, he didn't want to hear them and left."

"I have to go."

She grabbed her purse and drove to Tony's. When she arrived, she said a quick prayer that God would open his heart, and he would listen to what she had to say. Before she could knock, her phone pinged, and something told her not to ignore it.

"Not now, Anna," read the text. "Go away."

"Come on, Tony, you have to let me in," she yelled at the door. "I want to talk to you."

"Why?"

"You know why."

"I don't, Anna. I love you, but you don't trust me. All I want to do is help you through this hurt, but you keep pushing me away."

"I'm pushing everyone away!"

At that, he opened the door and walked away from it. Anna let herself in and shut it behind her.

"Not your mom. Not Gina."

"That's different. They're my girlfriends."

She noticed the smirk on his face at the mention of her mother as one of her girlfriends.

"Be real, Anna."

"I am. I felt elated to be talking to you again. What we have is still so fragile. Why would I want to ruin that by revealing what happened with Garrett? That he sent Erica over to try to get info about what he did to me? There was no point! But I had to vent to someone, so I went to them. Is that so wrong?"

"The point is when you love someone, you go to them with your problems. But then again, you never said those three words to me."

"Tony. It was all going so well before Garrett screwed everything up. And that's not my fault. I did nothing to deserve what he did to me. You need to cut me some slack and stop trying to fix me!"

It was almost like she could see the air get sucked

from his lungs.

"So that's it. You'll never forgive me for going to the pastor. For making sure that guy got what he deserved."

"It wasn't your battle to fight."

"Right. Cause you're doing such a stellar job fighting it."

His face fell immediately as the gravity of his words sunk in. "I'm sorry."

"It's fine."

"It's not. You didn't fight back in the beginning, but then you did, and you were ignored. I just wish you would keep fighting."

"He doesn't believe me, Tony. I can't make him."

"You can, Anna. Didn't telling Stella's story teach you anything? You have to keep applying the pressure. They can't get away with this!"

"Her story taught me that I'm lucky. I wasn't raped. I was pushed around by a big brawny guy, big deal. All I want to do is move on."

She knew he wasn't buying it. How could he, when clearly she was lightyears away from moving on. She had to get out of there. She declined to look at him because all she saw was a reminder of everything Garrett took from her.

"Listen, Tony, talking to you this past week was great. But this is proof that it's too soon."

"Don't do that." He grabbed her hand and pulled her to him, but she wouldn't allow herself to be drawn into his arms. She wasn't ready to face her situation, and they couldn't be together until she figured out what came next. She felt the tears well up and turned to leave before Tony could see her pain.

"I'm sorry, I'm not who you need me to be," were her last words before she left him alone.

~

Tony still reeled from Anna's words. She was everything he wanted. The fact that Anna questioned that was astonishing. When his dreams came at night or during the light of day, she was always there. He fantasized about their wedding, their children, and all the mundane things in between.

Tony fell to the ground and raised his hands to his head. "God, why do I keep messing up with her? Why do I keep pushing her? I know she is the one you have chosen for me. Tell me, Lord what to do."

Wait for her. Trust in Me.

~

Anna pulled out of Tony's driveway, somehow keeping the tears at bay. Her hand moved to her phone several times but pulled back. Who was she going to call? Her friends, her family? All of them would tell her she had to move on, that she was throwing away an amazing man. She knew all that, so she didn't need them making it worse.

~

A week passed since she saw Tony, and the hurt hadn't waned. If anything, she missed him more than she thought possible. And worse, she was utterly alone, as she wasn't responding to anyone—not even Gina. She was back to her despondent self at work, but the only thing that saved her, and her job, was that she was doing some of the best reporting of her life. Telling Stella's story ignited a fire in her, and now she was pouring all her frustrations into the paper. Dan had nothing to complain about, but he cared about her. She could see it in his eyes when he passed her desk each day, trying to get her to talk, but she always went right back to her computer, with excuses of having to meet his deadlines.

The emails were still coming from people thanking her for telling Stella's story, commending Stella for her bravery. With every email she read, she felt more like a failure. She wanted to push like Tony said—she did—but every time she thought of calling Pastor Tom again, fear gripped her like a vice. She tried to pray it away, but no matter what she did, the blinding panic was always there—of how Garrett would punish her if she fought back.

"Hey, Ace, come on, let's grab lunch. I'm not taking no for an answer."

She looked at Nico, trying to figure out if Dan sent him over, but she didn't care. She was hungry, and Nico didn't know about her demons. "Sounds good, let's go."

Anna looked at her half-eaten spicy Italian sandwich from her favorite deli down the road and wondered how she could be so stupid. She forgot that she introduced her co-worker to Tony at the game and that Nico reported on the team all the way to States. Anyone who came across Tony, even for a brief period, was drawn to him, and Nico was no different. He asked her all kinds of questions. What were the players up to? Who went to what college? What were Tony's thoughts about the next season? She tried to come off like they still talked, but Nico was a reporter too. He could see right through her.

"What happened, Anna?"

"I don't want to talk about it. But we aren't together

anymore."

"I'm sorry. He's a great guy."

"Don't you think I know that?" she said, raising her voice.

"Whoa! I'm sorry, Anna. I will stop. I promise."

"No, I'm sorry. I shouldn't have yelled at you."

"If you ever need someone to talk to, I'm here."

"No offense, Nico, but I have plenty of people who want me to open up about this. To get over a bunch of things that have happened to me. But I can't do that."

"You brought me here because I was safe. And then I went and asked you questions, just like everyone else. I'm sorry."

She laughed. "I will let you off the hook. You didn't do it on purpose. If you promise to not ask me about any of that, I would be happy to have lunch with you again."

"Wow, I must be pretty charming then. You got yourself a deal. No questions, I promise. I'll just turn on my witty personality. Because, when you let go, Anna, when you smile. When you laugh, everyone in the room is done for."

She willed back the tears and wondered when she would be able to have a conversation without turning on the waterworks.

"I didn't mean that in a creepy way, Anna." She raised her eyebrows at him. "I just mean that you have this light inside of you. Everyone sees it. And when all the pain dies down, and I promise you it will, I can't wait to see that light shine through brighter than ever."

A single tear started to fall, and she swiped it away.

"Thanks, Nico."

"Anytime, Ace."

They walked back to the office together, and before she started working again, she took out her phone. She was at war with herself on whether she should text Tony, but the pull was too strong. Anna knew she was playing a game of tug-of-war with his heart but couldn't stop herself.

"Hey, are you okay?" she typed.

"As good as I can be without my favorite girl."

The wistful smile appeared immediately, and she debated what to type back and decided to take the friends route.

"Nico asked a ton of questions about you today. I think there may be a bromance brewing there."

He sent back a laughing emoji right away.

"Tell him I said hey."

"Will do."

"Now it's my turn to ask. Are you okay?"

"As good as I can be without my favorite guy."

~

It had been at least a minute since Anna sent that last text, and he didn't know how to respond. But it told him there was hope. Over the past week, he convinced himself he had to cut ties with her. That his heart couldn't take this ping pong match anymore. But then God spoke to him again. *Wait for her.*

"I'll be here for you always," he texted back.

She sent back a simple heart, and he knew his dreams that night would be the stuff of fantasies.

Chapter 22

"You are sure she won't be mad at you?" Tony pestered Elizabeth again.

"Stop asking me, or I will change my answer," she yelled back at him through the phone.

"And now you are making me question myself. I don't know, Tony. She misses you, but she is still pretty screwed up. All I can say is that life is too short not to take risks. And you love this girl. So, man up and ask the woman to sit next to you in church. It's not a proposal."

He grinned through the phone at his friend and couldn't wait to be around when this feisty blonde spitfire met her match in a man.

"Okay, you convinced me. And that's my excuse to hang up on you so I can text her."

Tony knew he was taking the cowardly way out, but a man could only take so much rejection.

He was surprised when Anna replied back immediately that she would love for the three of them to attend church together on Sunday.

"She said, yes! Thanks, Liz," he typed.

"People should listen to me more. I'll get Anna, then swing by for you. See ya Sunday."

~

The sweat was glistening on his palms, and Tony

wasn't even sitting next to Anna. When they arrived at the church and Tony took his seat, he noticed her usher Elizabeth in next. Yes, it bothered him, but he tried to count the small blessings as they came. And here he was worshipping God with Anna only two seats away.

When the pastor began preaching, he was reminded how lucky they were to have found this church. He was a gifted speaker who matched Pastor Tom in both wisdom and delivery—they both kept his attention each week. If they had to be forced from a church, he was glad God placed this new one in their path. His next step was to convince the girls to check out their singles group. One step at a time, he reminded himself, then Tony shifted his focus back to the pastor's words.

"Let's talk about some myths we hear when our fellow Christians are trying to make us feel better. When the trials of this world have us so far in the pit that we swear we will never crawl out of the mud. 'God never gives us more than we can handle.' What a load of bunk. Who's with me, church?" A chorus of laughter and amens resounded through the sanctuary. "Did Joseph have more than he could handle when his brothers stripped him and left him for dead? Or when he was Potiphar's servant, and his wife attempted to seduce him? A case could be made for 'yes,' don't you think, church?" More laughter and amens reverberated.

"What did God do throughout that story? He brought Joseph out of the pit his brothers threw him in—literally—and into favor with Potiphar. In the end, Joseph enjoyed immense wealth and good fortune. But did Joseph see all that coming when his brothers turned on him? Of course, he didn't, church—but he prayed, and he stayed loyal to God, and he never stopped believing that God would deliver him. Now I wish I could promise all of you that your story will end like Joseph's. That you will end up with tremendous wealth, that you will be reunited with your family, and live a life of prosperity. I can't do that. But I'm here to tell you that God has you in the palm of His hand. Those sitting here right now who are weary and heavy-laden, God will provide rest, just as He says He will in Matthew Chapter 11.

"And some of you are thinking, pastor, I need that rest. I'm tired. I don't have any fight left in me. Remember Joshua Chapter 1, verses 9 and 10: Be strong and courageous. Do not be afraid; do not be discouraged, for the LORD your God will be with you wherever you go."

Although it was so slight, Tony knew the second Elizabeth reached over and put her hand on Anna's. He sensed the moment Anna reached up and swiped that lone tear away before it fell. And he knew that his precious girl was holding on by a thread.

"Let's bow our heads together. If you are sitting here feeling all alone, bring your cares before the Lord. If you are here today and need God's comforting hand on you, and if you want me to pray for you this week, simply look up at me now and nod."

Tony knew he shouldn't glance over, but the desire was too strong to ignore. This sermon was hitting close to home—and one Anna needed. So, he looked to his right, opened his eyes, and saw her lock eyes with the pastor. Like a kid about to be caught with his hand in the candy jar, he quickly bowed his head again, closed his eyes, and said his own prayer. "God, I know You have her. Bring her back to me in Your time."

When the pastor gave the final blessing, he physically restrained himself from going to Anna and pulling her into his arms. The three of them exited in silence, with Elizabeth walking slightly ahead. Maybe it was on purpose, but he was too worried about Anna to care. And perhaps that's why Tony couldn't recall when she took his hand in his. But when he noticed it when they were almost at the car, he wished she would never let him go.

~

Anna joined Gina on the couch, thankful her friend opted to hang out with her tonight. Not that it was hard to coax her over here. She loved her kids, but Anna knew Gina longed for regular girlfriend time. She wished she was ready to have the whole group together for a girls' night. Anna missed Grace and loved when they all gathered together. And she wanted to know if anything new was happening with Grace and her ex. At least she saw Elizabeth at church. Anna was even eager to invite Stella for one of their get-togethers. But for now, she relished the chance to catch up with her sweet sister-in-law. Gina grabbed a barbecue chip then launched in, "So what's the latest?"

Anna filled her in on the pastor's words, which both comforted and scared her. She didn't know if she could be strong and courageous. And she was still very much afraid, which left her right where she has been all along. Living in fear, avoiding her old church, and evading Tony most of the time, though he rarely left her thoughts.

"Wow, you never are at a loss for words, Gina. Now I'm scared."

"I'm just processing," she said with a smile.

"Care to share?"

"Anna, all I can say is I know with all my heart that you two will find your way back to each other. That God will work in this situation—and that includes exposing Garrett. I don't know how or when, but I am confident He will. But don't leave me hanging. So, you held Tony's hand after church. What happened in the few days since then?"

"Nothing. I haven't reached out, and neither has he."

"You know it has to be you, Anna. No offense, but you have sent him mixed signals."

"You're right. I need to get my act together. I'm still annoyed that he meddled, even though I shouldn't be. I try to stay away, but when I see him, my middle turns to mush."

"Why did you take his hand that day?"

She didn't even hesitate. "Because Tony makes me feel safe."

"Maybe you should grab on to that, Anna."

"But if I stay away from him, maybe I will get over him. That's why I'm not texting."

"But you're hoping he reaches out to you, don't you?"

"Yes! What is wrong with me?"

"You're in love."

"Enough about me. What's the latest with my mother? She has been strangely quiet, and that is terrifying."

"Well, I don't know that you need to be terrified, but your mom and dad are worried about you. They are thrilled you have been coming around to dinners more, but you are their daughter. And I'm pretty sure your dad wants to run into Garrett in a dark alley."

She knew the comment was designed to make her smile, but anytime Garrett's name came up, all she felt was disgust and shame.

"I'm sorry, Anna."

"Don't be. Let's talk about something else. How are the kids?"

"Amazing. AJ asked about you the other day. He wants his Aunt Anna to come see him."

"Tell him I love him, and I will spoil him on Sunday."

"Will do. And Eva is getting bigger than ever, and she laughs and giggles all the time now. It brings me such joy."

"You deserve it. And my brother?"

"As doting as ever."

"Blech. I'll take your word for it."

"He keeps waiting for you and Tony to get back together so we can double-date."

Anna sighed heavily. She tried not to picture it, but all she did was fantasize about her future with Tony. Of family dinners, double dates, baseball games, lazy days at the beach. She even let her mind wander to marriage and kids. She wanted it all with him, but it was too late for that now.

"Come on, let's get your mind off all this and watch our movie." Anna hoped the romantic comedy wouldn't bring thoughts of Tony in her head. Who was she kidding? He was always in her thoughts—and her heart.

~

It was Friday now. Five days had passed since the hand-holding, as her friends referred to it, and she still hadn't talked to Tony. She filed a story, and Dan told

231

her to enjoy the weekend, so she decided to grab a coffee before she figured out how to spend the rest of her day. She walked into Peet's Coffee and noticed Erica immediately. The girl looked like she hadn't slept in days and acted like a caged animal, with her eyes darting all around, looking for what Anna didn't know, nor did she want to. In fact, she tried to run the other way, but Erica jumped up to meet her.

"I was waiting for you."

Anna looked at her with shock.

"I mean, I know this is by your office, and you come in here a lot. I figured if I texted or called, you would ignore me."

Erica's eyes darted around the room again. "Don't worry, he won't see us. He's at a competition this weekend."

"Why would I be worried that he would see us, Erica?"

"I know he did something to you, Anna. He hurt me too."

Anna still didn't trust her, but now the girl captured her attention.

"Let's sit down. You look like you are going to jump out of your skin."

Erica sat but fidgeted endlessly. She dove right in with questions for Anna. "I saw you here with that girl, Stella, who was raped. I can tell you had a connection with her, and I know Garrett did something to you. Did he rape you? Is that why you wanted to tell Stella's story?"

"No! Did he rape you, Erica?"

"I stopped him."

Her voice was devoid of emotion when she said it.

232

Was this what Anna looked like to others? She couldn't analyze that now. She had to figure out what happened to the frightened person in front of her.

"Erica, I still don't trust you. I don't know if you will use what I am about to tell you against me. But I am done hiding." Then she laid out everything between her and Garrett and how the pastor turned a blind eye. Erica was quiet for a good minute, which had Anna uneasy and unsure what to do next.

"So, you told the pastor what Garrett did to you, and he looked the other way? If he would have done something, maybe it would have stopped Garrett from hitting me. Do I have that right?"

She said it all without an ounce of emotion. "We can't know what the pastor would have done, but yes, I would like to think that two incidents would make him investigate this. And at least get Garrett off stage each week and booted from the payroll."

"Aren't you mad, Anna?"

It seemed like such an easy question, but she didn't know how to answer it. So many emotions overwhelmed her in the past few months: sadness, loss of hope in people to do the right thing, betrayal, loss. She named all those emotions for Erica, and the girl took her hand.

"I'm so sorry, Anna. I could have helped you, and I didn't. You should be angry with me at least."

"No apology is needed, Erica, but I appreciate you saying that. Garrett fooled a lot of us. But, you know what? Now that I know your story, I am angry. And I think we need to fight back and pray that the Lord will be with us."

"I was hoping you would say that. You are right,

but I can't do it alone."

Anna squeezed Erica's hand. "You won't. Are you ready to talk details, or do you need more time?"

"I'm ready," she said while pulling up something on her phone. "And I have photos of my injuries."

Anna sucked in a breath as she examined the bruises on Erica's arms and legs, and she felt a few tears running down her cheek.

"I'm sorry this happened to you."

Erica gave her a weak smile. "So, what is our first step? The pastor?"

"Not yet. I don't see how he could ignore these, but I no longer have confidence Pastor Tom will help. I'm jaded now—that's what Garrett did to us—what the church did to us, Erica."

"It sounds like you are getting a little angry now."

"I am. And that's why we are confiding in someone I trust with my life. Let's go."

Chapter 23

Anna looked at her dad with his head in his hands and realized he wanted to punch something—or someone. When he studied those photos, his heart broke for Erica, but she was certain he saw Anna in them as well. And that's why she knew he would do whatever he had to, to make sure Garrett never hurt anyone again. Anna was ready to fight now and would do whatever her father recommended.

Erica was the one who spoke first. "Sir, are we going to the pastor?"

Anna sensed the fear in her voice and knew her father heard it also.

"Garrett broke the law, Erica. He hurt you. He hurt my daughter too, but we don't have proof of that. But you do. If you file a restraining order against him, that will set off a chain reaction, then the police can monitor him. It's bigger than the church now, honey. Believe me, I will deal with that later, but for now, we have to take steps to keep you and other women safe."

"Will you both be there with me?

"Every step," Anna answered.

"I'm proud of both of you," said John. "And I will be there to help you through this. When does Garrett get back from his competition?"

"Two days—Sunday night."

"Then let's go down to the station and start the paperwork."

Erica and Anna rose, but John stopped them.

"I'm not trying to scare you, but I need to keep you both safe. Would you mind staying here for a few days, especially when Garrett comes home? I don't want him going to look for you, Erica."

"Believe me, I don't want that either."

"It's settled then. Let's go to the station, then we will drive to your apartments to get what you need."

~

So much happened in the last two days. The restraining order was filed. Anna was on edge, but she also possessed a sense of calm. She finally allowed people to help her. She looked around at those gathered at the table for Sunday dinner, her parents, Gina, Christian, the kids, and Erica. Anna watched Erica look at the clock several times throughout dinner. She knew it was a ticking time bomb and that she only had a few hours until Garrett came home from his tournament. John said he was sending an officer over around nine to serve him the restraining order papers. Until then, they would wait. But Anna now felt safe in her home and knew she had people around to protect her—except the one person she really wanted here. She had almost called him so many times, and her family chastised her constantly in the past few days for not reaching out to Tony. Something always stopped her—namely guilt. She didn't let him in before, so why now? Mostly she was paralyzed by fear—that he viewed her as weak and not the person he fell in love with. She knew it made no sense, especially when he kept telling her how much he cared for her. But she was ashamed—and she hated that she let Garrett change her.

Her mom interrupted her thoughts. "Anna, can you run out and grab the mail—the neighbor said she left something in the box for me."

"Sure, Mom."

She stepped on the porch and lost her breath. Tony looked so handsome, and she memorized the sight of him. The barely-there stubble, the red t-shirt that complemented his dark hair perfectly. His strong arms that she was dying to be pulled into. And then the shame hit. He knew everything now. She didn't know which family member told him, but he was likely hurt Anna didn't tell him herself. Just another way she disappointed this man she loved so much.

"I'm proud of you, Anna."

And that was all it took for the flood gates to open and the messy tears to flow. Then he pulled her into his arms, her head flush against his firm chest, and whispered soothing words in her ear while she poured out all the stress of the past few months. She finally drew back and gestured for him to sit next to her in one of the porch chairs but never let go of his hand.

"I have a lot of things to tell you, and just let me get them out."

He nodded and squeezed her hand.

"I'm sorry I pushed you away. I'm sorry I was angry that you went to the pastor. I know now that none of that was about you. It was my stubbornness that got the best of me."

"You, stubborn?"

She swatted him playfully and continued.

"You have to understand that all of this came from shame. Shame that I was lured in by Garrett's looks and

237

charm. Shame that I pushed you away when you wanted to help. Shame that I wasn't acting like the Godly person I wanted to be. And there was anger too. A lot of anger. At God for letting this happen to me when I was falling for you. And a lot of anger at the church for not protecting me."

"I know, Anna. And that's why I waited for you. Why I will always wait for you. I know you didn't mean to push me away. I pray for you every day, you know—for us."

"So, God brought me back to you."

"God brought you back to me."

~

Tony had never experienced such relief and panic all at the same time. After their conversation on the porch, Anna led him into the house by the hand and barely let him go. It felt amazing to be around this family again—it was tense, but there was also a lot of laughter. But now that it was 9:30, and John had confirmation that the order had been served, they were all on edge. Erica kept looking at her phone, then they all heard the ding.

"Read it aloud, Erica," said John.

"Where are you?"

"I went away for a few days," she typed back, just as they had rehearsed earlier.

"Did you know about this?" he texted.

"Know about what?"

"Don't play dumb me with me."

"Garrett, I don't know what you are talking about. Did you lose or something? Is that why you are in a bad mood?"

Erica said the words aloud as she typed them. When

she read those last sentences, John warned her.

"Remember what we talked about, Erica. Do not provoke him."

"Is he typing anything back?" Tony asked.

"No, he is smart enough to not get mean in a text, as he knows that can be used against him. I can picture him pacing around his apartment, furious as ever."

"That's what we want, Erica. He will feel desperate and make a mistake. And we will be there to catch him."

She nodded, and Tony relaxed in the knowledge that Erica and Anna were finally allowing others to help them.

"Before we all try to get some sleep, I have to tell you something, and you may not be happy. But it's what's best for you two, and if you are mad at me, then so be it."

Tony observed the two girls' eye John warily.

"Tomorrow morning, Pastor Tom is coming here. He needs to know how far this goes."

They both rose from their chairs simultaneously and embraced John in a hug and murmured words of thanks. Tony prayed this nightmare would soon be over. Anna sat down again next to Tony and looked at him. "Will you be here tomorrow with me?"

"Tomorrow and always."

A collective aww went around the room, and they all laughed.

"That's it. No one is going to bed yet," Helena announced. "I think we all need some late-night dessert. Who's in?"

All the hands went up, and Tony couldn't wait until he was part of this wonderful family forever.

~

Tony entered the spacious living room of the Andros home and looked around at Anna and Erica, then John and Helena. The two girls were almost one as they sat close to each other with their arms clasped together. He walked over to them, took the seat next to Anna, and gave her a kiss on the cheek, then leaned over to speak to both of them.

"Remember, God's got you."

They both smiled, then the doorbell rang, and the tension in the room returned. John told them last night that he told Pastor Tom very little. He simply said they needed to talk about his daughter Anna Andros—as the two men had never even met.

Pastor Tom walked into the room, and everyone exchanged polite hellos. Though it lasted only a second, it was evident he registered surprise at seeing Erica there.

"Have a seat, Pastor," said John. "I'm sure you know Anna is the reason I brought you here today. She told you of something that happened with an employee of yours, and you did nothing to look into it."

Pastor Tom opened his mouth to speak, but John silenced him with his hand. "I don't know what possible reason you could have for not investigating such damning claims from a church member. No reason you try to tell me will make me feel better, so let's just skip that part. I want to show you what your inaction caused, and this time you need to fix it."

Erica rose from the couch, and Tony saw Anna squeeze her hand before letting go. Then she handed Pastor Tom her phone. "This is what Garrett did to me."

Everyone watched him wince when he saw the

photos. Then they simply waited. It was on him now to take these crucial next steps.

"I'm so sorry, Anna. Erica. I failed you both as a pastor. But frankly, I didn't even act like a decent human being. I'm going to ask for forgiveness, but I don't expect you to accept it. I'm not sure I would if I were you. I have no right to ask anything of you, but can we pray?"

Both girls nodded their heads, then the group came joined in an impromptu circle and held hands.

"Dear Lord, I come to you now acknowledging my sins. I have committed a severe offense against Anna and Erica, and for that, I am deeply sorry. I pray for them right now, that you will take away their pain and suffering, that you will bring Garrett to justice, and that one day they will trust people again—the church, myself, and others who let them down. I thank you for putting loving people around them who helped them through this. I pray for their continued peace and healing. In your precious name, we pray. Amen."

Tony heard the chorus of amens around the room, then saw the tears running down his girl's cheek. He grabbed her hand and squeezed and pulled her into him. She settled into him like a glove—it was a perfect fit—and he wasn't letting her go this time.

John rose to meet the pastor and shake his hand. "Thank you for coming and for doing the right thing."

He simply nodded, as it was evident he was still reeling from everything that happened this morning.

"I will be ending his employment today. Are you girls staying here for a while?"

"I will take care of them, Pastor," said John.

He nodded, said goodbye to Helena, and walked out

the door.

~

Two weeks later, Anna and Erica were back living in their apartments. Still, John took precautions in case Garrett was dumb enough to show up. He installed security cameras at both of their residences—highly visible ones. He wanted Garrett to know he was being watched.

Tony looked across the table at John and admired him for taking care of his family. He wanted to be that man one day. To protect those around him. His gaze continued across the room for those who had joined this wonderful brood. Stella and her mom were here, Erica, Elizabeth, and Grace, in addition to the family. Tony couldn't remember ever being so happy. All of that had to do with the woman seated by his side. Anna's hand rested on his arm, where it had been most of the day. John's booming voice brought him out of his thoughts as he stood.

"It's time for me to get sentimental and to share some news."

All eyes were on John, even little AJ, who sat still in his seat. "I thank God for my family gathered here today and our extended family—which is all of you. We met some of you through heartache, but I think that was part of God's plan. We needed to encounter each other to heal. I know it's still a long road ahead for some of you, but I look at you, I see your smiles, I see the support you have here, and I know you are going to be okay. As Tony says, 'God's got you.'"

Helena swiped a tear from her perfectly made-up face and squeezed her husband's hand. Again, Tony yearned for this—all of it.

John continued. "I also have some news from Pastor Tom to share. It may be hard to hear, but you all are strong, and I know you can handle it." He looked directly at Erica, then at Anna. Both girls nodded, signifying for John to continue.

"Pastor Tom called me this week with an update. Garrett is no longer employed at the church. My sources also tell me he has moved out of his apartment. You girls still need to be aware, but I am confident you are safe. Garrett can't hurt you any longer."

Now, most of the people in the room were wiping their eyes.

"But there's more. Pastor Tom knows you found a new church, but he wants you to consider coming to First United this Sunday. The decision is totally up to you both, but if you decide to go, this whole group will be with you."

Erica and Anna exchanged confused glances, and Tony saw that John noticed it too.

"Your guess is as good as mine, girls. I don't know why he wants you there. The decision is yours."

Chapter 24

The Andros clan and their friends occupied a full row at church. Anna looked around and knew that whatever happened today, she was blessed beyond measure. Still, the sweat beads were forming under her arms, and the unknown overwhelmed her. She decided to put it in God's hands, so she squeezed Tony's arm then leaned in so only he could hear her, "God's got this."

"That's my girl," then she placed the lightest of kisses on his cheek and watched the smile rise to his ears. He loved her, and she reveled in that and was looking forward to telling him the same sometime soon. But first, she had to get through today.

The pastor's sermon was all about listening to the voice of God. He went through practical ways to do that, from praying to journaling to reading the Bible daily. Anna looked at the rapt faces around her and saw many people taking notes and nodding their heads in affirmation. If Pastor Tom hadn't disappointed her so much, she would have been doing the same. The anger rose up inside her again, and her knee started to shake.

"You okay?" Tony whispered.

"I don't know. I kind of want to get out of here."

"I'll do whatever you need."

She looked up at that moment, locked eyes with

Pastor Tom, and sensed he knew exactly what she was thinking. Then he walked away from his notes, from the pulpit, and spoke right to her.

"Church, I come to you today with a heavy heart. I just told you all about listening to the voice of God, but that's the thing. He will talk to you, but what do you do when you don't like the answer? Well, don't ignore Him like I did. I have to confess my sins, church. I had someone come to me for my help, but it fell on deaf ears. But the thing is, looking back, I know the Lord was telling me to help this person, but I ignored Him. Why? Because it would have been uncomfortable for me. Do you believe that? So, you know what happened by my inaction? Someone else got hurt. I don't know if that pain and regret will ever ease. I ask the people I have wronged to forgive me. I ask you all to forgive me for not being the man God wants me to be. And I implore you to listen when God speaks to you. It may be wonderful, but it may be wildly uncomfortable. But take it from me. You need to listen."

The band then took their place on the stage, a mid-forties-ish woman as the worship leader now, and Anna looked over at Erica. Her new friend nodded back to her, and they headed to the back of the church toward the exit. Although Anna never saw him leave, she knew Tony followed behind her. They were that in sync now, and she knew he would never abandon her. As soon as Erica and Anna arrived at the car, hand-in-hand, they collapsed into each other's arms.

~

Tony stood there, watching these two strong women comfort each other. They needed this time alone, but he was mesmerized by their strength through this situation.

He felt the presence of others and was soon flanked by their whole crew of friends and family.

"What are you doing over here?" joked Elizabeth, nudging his arm playfully. "Go to her."

"Yeah, what are you doing over there?" yelled Anna. He moved in long fast strides and reached her within seconds, pulled her into his arms and into a kiss. Their friends cheered then headed over to the girls, and it was a flurry of hugs and laughter.

"Well, this seems like the one time to ditch Sunday dinner in favor of Sunday brunch," said Helena. "Let's go. I need to start prepping."

They all laughed, and Tony watched John walk to Anna. He was close enough to hear their words.

"You okay?"

"I really am. You're not going to make me talk to him, though, are you?"

"Of course not, Anna. I'm proud of the pastor for owning up to what he did before his entire congregation. But you don't owe him anything."

"Thanks, Dad."

~

The doorbell rang, and Anna practically raced to the door so girls' night could commence. The whole group would be here, Grace, Elizabeth, Stella, Erica, and, of course, Gina. Once they all settled in with their food and drinks, all eyes landed on Anna.

"What?"

"Oh, come on, Anna. Tell us!" said Elizabeth.

"Tell you what?" she replied, feigning ignorance.

That's when Stella threw a pillow at her.

"Oh, I like you," said Elizabeth. "You will fit in here just fine."

"Stop, don't encourage her," Anna teased back.

"They are right," said Grace. "Why are you so coy? Have you told that poor boy you love him yet?"

The blush crept all the way up her cheeks. "Not yet, but I have a plan."

"You're not going to tell us what it is, are you?" asked Elizabeth.

Anna exchanged a look with Gina, and she knew Liz saw it—that girl misses nothing.

"You know!"

"I'm not saying a word. Sister-in-law pact is in place."

"Well, when is this grand event happening?" asked Stella.

"Friday night."

"Then I declare a Saturday morning brunch to get all the details."

They all laughed and promised to be there but vowed they would be at the edge of their seats with excitement until then.

~

Tony wiped his palms for the umpteenth time as he stood outside Anna's apartment. All she told him was to come with an appetite, but he had no idea how he could eat, with all the butterflies moving around in his mid-section. He had no idea why he was nervous, but he sensed this would be a special night. That's why he brought the flowers in his hand, her favorite—lilies.

He went to dry his palms on his pants once more when the door opened. "Are you going to stand out here all day, or are you going to come in for our date?"

Her beauty literally took his breath, and he fought to find words. "You are beautiful."

"Why, thank you."

She was wearing one of those sundresses he loved so much. This one went right to her knees and was full of vibrant blues and greens that brought out the sparkle in her eyes. Her hair, usually flowing to her shoulders or in a ponytail, was piled on her head in a loose bun. He resisted the urge to reach out and brush away the tendrils framing her face. Her eyes darted to the flowers, making him realize how nervous he was. "Sorry, these are for you."

"Thank you. What's the occasion?"

"Dinner with you."

She smiled, and he was surprised when she didn't usher him inside.

"Well, it is a special occasion, you know?"

He raised his eyebrows.

"It's me, wanting to make you feel special like you do for me every day. It's me recreating a night that went so wrong when I wanted it to go so right. So, welcome to our new beginning."

He looked inside, and there went his breath again. Anna had recreated that picnic from that day they all wanted to erase. The blanket on the ground was full of Italian delights from olives to cheese, to salami, homemade bread, cannoli, and more."

"This is amazing," he said while tugging her into him, his arms sliding around her waist. "Thank you."

"You're welcome. I have all your favorites. I even snagged some recipes from your mom."

The thought of Anna and his mom swapping recipes made his stomach flip again. He knew they were now on the road back together, that they still had a lot of dating to do, but when it came to Anna, he couldn't stop thinking about their future. He was so sure of it, pictured it so clearly that he had to stop and remind himself to go slow with her. That she was still healing. He felt her hand take his, knocking him out of his thoughts and leading him to the blanket.

"I'm serving you, Mr. Donelli, so what shall it be?"

"That's easy. Everything!"

As they sat and enjoyed the delicacies Anna prepared, he was in awe of how easy the conversation flowed. This was how it was before Garrett screwed it all up.

"You're thinking of him, aren't you?"

He shouldn't have been surprised by her words. It only reminded him of how in sync they were.

"I'm sorry. This is so amazing. All of this. I can't help it. My mind just flashed to the months we lost."

"You have to let it go, Tony."

They both looked at each other and erupted into laughter.

"I know it's ridiculous that I'm saying those words to you. I am the one who let Garrett control me for the past few months and affect our relationship. But I have let it go. And I beg you to do the same."

He nodded his head, moved their plates to the side, and lightly pressed his lips to hers. He went to deepen the kiss, and she pulled away, and he chastised himself silently for going too fast.

She waved her hand across the room. "This is my way of starting over. That night, I had so many things planned for us."

"Like?"

She shook her head. "Before I go there, I have to say I'm sorry."

"Anna, there's nothing."

She interrupted him firmly.

"There is."I pushed you away. I'm so sorry I blamed you when all you were trying to do was help me, protect me. In fact, that's one of the things I love about you so much."

All her other words faded into the background. One of the things she loved about him. Did she love him? He watched her close the distance until there was only a breath separating them.

"I love you, Tony. I planned to tell you that night. Even though I didn't act like it, I have loved you all these months."

Tony could barely breathe. Now that she said the words he wanted to hear so badly, he wondered if this was another dream. The one he had every single night they were apart. Would he wake up to find her gone? Or did God listen to his prayers and bring them back together?

"Tony?"

He saw the tears pooling in her eyes, and he realized this was real. He closed the smallest of distances and put his lips to hers for barely a few seconds. Then he pulled back and wiped her tears. "I love you, Anna Andros. And I am never letting you go."

Epilogue

"Tell me I'm not crazy."

"Anna, stop it. We've been over this," said Grace.

"It's practically the most romantic thing I've ever heard of," said Elizabeth, feigning disdain. Anna knew her friend all too well. She acted like she didn't want any of the happily ever after, but all the girls knew she did. Anna just had to figure out why she was holding back. Maybe Gina could help with that. They had been best friends since college. She brought herself back into reality—figuring out Liz's emotional issues were a problem for another day. Today was all about her and Tony.

"Hey, Christian's proposal to me was pretty great," said Gina.

"Sorry, didn't mean to leave you out. Yes, you also have the most romantic relationship--and one of the few good guys out there."

"Oh my gosh, enough with the 'woe is me,'" said Stella. "You are funny and beautiful, and I see the way all the guys look at you. People like me would die for your confidence."

"What?" Anna blurted while putting the finishing touches on her hair. "You have confidence in spades, girl."

"I fought back. There's a difference. I still hurt

every day, and there is nothing I can do to erase that shame and move on."

Elizabeth strode to Stella with her big heart on her sleeve and pulled her into a hug. She whispered something in her ear, and Anna was dying to know what it was. She knew Gina was curious too, but not today. Elizabeth would reveal the details when the time was right. If she shared a moment and kinship with their new friend, they should let them have that.

"Why on earth are you fixing your hair to go paddleboarding?" asked Gina.

"Because she wants everything to be perfect," said Grace, like the true Southern woman that she was. "There will be pictures from today, you know. Our girl has to look her best."

"She could be wearing a burlap sack, and that guy wouldn't take his eyes off her," said Stella.

Anna smiled, knowing it was true. In the months since she and Tony had come back together, they were practically inseparable. From baseball games to gatherings with both their families, to double dates with Gina and Christian, hanging out with all of her friends—old and new, she was blissfully happy. And that was all because of Tony. She shouldn't second-guess herself. Tony had been going slow with her, with good reason. He was letting her set the pace, which was understandable after everything that happened between them. But she wanted to move forward with him, and today she was determined to make that happen. And she was going to do it where their relationship started to blossom—on the water.

~

"Why are you so nervous, man?" said Christian, for

what felt to Tony like the millionth time.

"If you do it right, you only propose once in your life. He has to get it right," said John.

"Yes, sir."

"My daughter is going to say yes in a second. We all know that," stated Helena, walking into the room, looking around for something to fix or straighten. Seeing none, she honed in on Tony. "You look quite handsome. Perfect for spending the day on the water— and of course, proposing to my daughter."

"Where is Gina today?" asked Helena, as if suddenly remembering she was nowhere to be found.

"Running some errands," said Christian.

Tony looked on as Helena raised her eyebrows at her son, then paced around the room. If she didn't stop, she was going to make him nervous.

"Okay, let's go over the plan again," she said, needing to have control, as Tony knew was her specialty. "You pick her up and go paddleboarding, then when you get back on the beach, you text us to head over. So, we'll be there right after you propose."

"Yes, Mom," he's got it," said Christian, and Tony was thankful to his future brother-in-law for saving him.

"Alright, Tony, then you go put a ring on my daughter's finger." Then she pulled him into a hug and whispered, "Welcome to the family," into his ear.

Tony navigated his truck into the lot, and although he wasn't nervous before, he definitely was now. Anna was uncharacteristically quiet on the way over here like she had something on her mind, which had him on edge. Was she ready for this? Was he going too fast?

This is My plan for you.

He said a silent prayer thanking God for those words that he sorely needed. And for reminding him that he prayed for their relationship all this time. It was meant to be, and he decided to ground himself in that fact as he went to open her door.

"Always the gentleman," she said with a smile, immediately giving him confidence again.

~

All the worries Anna carried with her on the drive melted away on the water. This was her happy place, and with Tony by her side, it was heaven.

"Want to float for a while?" he asked.

"You read my mind," she said, immediately crouching on her board then lying on her back to take in the sun.

With her eyes closed, she felt him take her hand as he floated next to her.

"You know this is where our relationship deepened," she said.

"That's why I'm so happy here. Though I'm happy anywhere with you, Anna."

She squeezed his hand, then moved her thumb up and down his palm as she talked.

"Me too, that's why I wanted to come out here with you. Do you know what today is?"

"Six months since our first trip on the water together." She jerked her eyes open and turned toward him.

"You remember that?"

"Of course. If you didn't invite me out here today, I was planning on asking you."

"We really are perfect together, you know."

"I do."

"Sorry, I was such a dunce for a bit there."

"I've forgiven you," he said playfully.

Should she do it now? She had it all planned for when they got back to the beach. The blanket, the wine. Her thoughts tumbled in a million directions, and she didn't know which ones to listen to.

"What's wrong?"

"Nothing. Do you want to head back?"

"Not really, but maybe we should. Want to hang out on the beach for a little before we head home?"

"Duh?" she teased before splashing water at him with her foot.

When they returned to the beach, Anna grabbed the blanket and saw Tony look at his phone, type something, and swipe something from his bag.

This was it. It seemed like such a good idea at the time. Her being the one proposing to prove how much she wanted to be with him. Anna was about to take his hand when he moved first and pulled her on the blanket next to him.

"Anna, you know I love you with all my heart."

She nodded.

"I'm not sure you know this next part. I prayed for us almost from the moment I developed feelings for you that went past friendship. I prayed when things were great and developing between us. And I prayed like crazy when things were falling apart. And that's when I felt the most peace. God told me he would take care of you, take care of us. He revealed His plan to me that we had a future together. I want a future with you, Anna."

"I want that too. In fact ..."

"Wait, I have to get this all out."

She moved closer to him, almost so she didn't miss a word, so she could touch him, feel the emotion pouring out of him, so he could sense the love flowing out of her soul at this moment.

"I want forever. I want to be a family; I want kids with you. I want it all."

Tears trickled down her cheeks, and before she wiped them away, he reached over, and with the slightest of touches, he erased them from her skin. The heat from his palm still burned. Then she saw him reach in his pocket, pull out a box, and she lost her breath. He pushed himself up on one knee and stole the question she thought she would be popping today.

"Will you marry me?"

"A thousand times yes!"

Then she leaped into his arms and delivered a kiss that she hoped spoke volumes. He pulled her from him, and before she could question why she saw her family and friends running to her. AJ got there first and proudly handed her a balloon that said, "Congratulations, you're engaged."

"He told you all?"

"Of course," her dad answered. "A gentleman still asks for the father's permission."

She looked at Gina, Elizabeth, Grace, and Stella and silently asked if they knew of Tony's plans. They all nodded their heads yes.

"What's going on here?" asked Tony. "All of you look like you have some big secret."

"We do," they all shouted.

"Tell him, Anna," said Gina.

She turned toward her fiancé and took his hand. "I pushed you away, Tony, and you have been going slow with me, which I appreciate. I wanted to do something bold to show you how much I love you, how much I want to move on with you. To build a family with you."

He looked at her quizzically.

"You beat me to it."

"To what?"

"To proposing," shouted Christian.

He looked at her, and she saw a few tears, and he closed the distance, and she immediately wiped them away.

"You were going to propose to me?"

She nodded.

He started laughing, "God really does have a plan. And a sense of humor."

If you loved this book, please go to Amazon, Gooodreads, or BookBub to leave a review.

Go to http://www.tarataffera.com to sign up for my newsletter.

Want to get a free short story, a prequel to Gina's first love? Click here to receive it now for free. And if you haven't read book one in the series, Love Ordained, get it here.

Read on for a preview of book three in a Divine Love Series. Coming in spring 2022.

If one more person told her how beautiful she looked, how it would be her turn to find love soon, Elizabeth was sure to run screaming from the room. But even that was impossible. She was at the wedding of two of her best friends and served as a bridesmaid. Her eyes found Tony and Anna swaying to the music, their gazes not wavering from the other. She knew those two would eventually get together, and she was thrilled to be a part of their big day. Elizabeth turned slightly, and now Gina and Christian were in her line of sight. She felt her heart melt at the sight of Christian leaning over, whispering in his wife's ear and gently pressing a tender kiss to her cheek. Two kids hadn't lessened their love story. If anything, it bloomed more each day.

She felt someone standing next to her, was relieved

to see it was Grace, and visibly let out her breath.

"Thank God it's you."

"Well, I love you too, sugar, but I didn't know I was your favorite."

Elizabeth nudged her playfully in the arm. "You're the only one here who won't tell me not to worry, that I will find love soon. Or to say, 'Why is someone so beautiful as you still single?'"

"Well, you know ..."

"Grace!   Not   you   too!" "You don't need to be married or have a boyfriend, Liz. You are strong and fearless, and every one of us envies and admires you. And yes, you tell us you don't need a boyfriend. But I'm good at reading people, honey, and I'm not buying what you're selling."

Elizabeth knew she couldn't fool Grace or any of her friends for that matter. But she vowed a long time ago to never reveal her past. Those skeletons were buried so far in the back of her closet, she refused to dig them out. She would continue to vow that love wasn't for her. One day they would believe her. No one could ever uncover the truth.

Grace no longer pushed. They simply stood observing their friends and reveling in their happiness. Still, Elizabeth felt the beads of perspiration appear under her arms. Grace's silence was almost as unnerving as her questions. Elizabeth watched as a distinguished man in his fifties swayed over to them, confidence exuding from his core. "May I have this dance?" he asked Grace.

"Go," said Elizabeth. "I'm good."

Grace squeezed her arm and walked away. Elizabeth exited quickly from the room, grateful for the cool air that greeted her. Or as cool it could be on a May night in Florida. Her eyes moved to two men talking several feet away. A man leaned on the deck rail, and his build and demeanor all seemed somehow familiar. That's when she knew she was losing it. Her mind dredged up the past, and now her imagination ran wild. She sat on the couch and couldn't help but overhear the conversation. It was evident the two men were father and son—their eyes, their mannerisms, all gave it away. The discussion centered around faith, and she felt a pang of jealousy—of conversations she would never have with her own family. Their voices were muffled, but she sensed the young man made some mistakes, learned from them, and desperately wanted to find a woman to love. Speaking of love, she knew it was time to get back to the wedding. Before she could stand to leave, Anna and Gina from the door to gain her attention.

At the mention of her name, the young man, who paid her no mind until now, turned to look, and Elizabeth felt her legs go limp. Please don't faint. Don't react. Then she turned away from the skeletons and toward her friends—her family—her lifeline. Away from the past, she thought she was outrunning so well.

Author Bio

Tara Taffera is a journalist living in Stafford, Va., with her husband of 23 years and three daughters. In 2020, she realized her dream of writing her first novel, Love Ordained, the first in a Christian romance series, A Divine Love. The series is based in Tarpon Springs, Florida, a small Greek town where Taffera lived for about three years as a young girl. She loved it so much that she made it the setting for her story. In July 2021, she visited and had so much fun touring the city again and earning additional ideas for the series.

Tara has always devoured books, and anyone who knows her knows how fast she can plow through a good novel. Her mother says she always asked to go back to the library for more books as a youngster. Thank goodness she has now discovered the Kindle and has a great story always within reach.

Follow Me on Social Media
https://www.facebook.com/authortarataffera
https://twitter.com/TaraTaffera
https://www.instagram.com/tarataffera/
https://www.goodreads.com/author/show/21190784
.Tara_Taffera
https://www.bookbub.com/profile/tara-taffera
https://www.linkedin.com/in/tara-taffera-b092545/
https://www.pinterest.com/ttaffera/
https://www.tiktok.com/@tarataffera

Made in the USA
Columbia, SC
19 January 2022